I0661117

Mrs. Campbell Praed

Mrs. Tregaskiss

A novel of Anglo-Australian life. Part 3

Mrs. Campbell Praed

Mrs. Tregaskiss
A novel of Anglo-Australian life. Part 3

ISBN/EAN: 9783337045760

Printed in Europe, USA, Canada, Australia, Japan

Cover: Foto ©Andreas Hilbeck / pixelio.de

More available books at **www.hansebooks.com**

MRS. TREGASKISS

A NOVEL OF ANGLO-AUSTRALIAN LIFE

BY

MRS. CAMPBELL PRAED

AUTHOR OF
'POLICY AND PASSION,' 'CHRISTINA CHARD,' 'THE ROMANCE OF
A STATION,' ETC.

IN THREE VOLUMES
VOL. III.

LONDON
CHATTO & WINDUS, PICCADILLY
1896

CONTENTS OF VOL. III.

CHAPTER XXIII.

JUST A MAN !

GENESTE and Clare had ridden almost in silence for some miles. The heat was very great, though the sun was not high, and he could not see her face, swathed as it was in her gray veil. She was riding a horse of his—one he had brought over from Darra with an ulterior view to rides with her—and while they were on the plain he mainly occupied himself in pacing the animal. But by-and-by they got into the gidia scrub, where there was less glare.

'I wish you would put up your veil,' he said. 'I know you are above small vanities; and besides, I know, too, that yours is the sort of skin which doesn't sun-burn easily.'

She did as he wished; then he fancied that under the shelter of her veil she had been crying.

'Don't be sad,' he said in that caressing voice which was his greatest charm with women. 'We have got a long, good day before us, and a delightful ride in the dusk to Darra. Let us try to forget that there is anything in the world to make us un-happy.'

She took no notice of the appeal.

'I want you to confess something truly to me,' she said seriously; 'you need not be afraid that I shall be jealous or hurt. Per-haps I am above those small vanities too. Tell me, did you ever really give Helen Cusack cause to think that you cared for her?'

'Frankly,' he replied, 'if it hadn't been for that meeting with you at Cedar Hill, and the revelation you gave me of your real self the night we camped by The Grave, I think it is more than likely I might now be engaged to Helen Cusack. Do you utterly despise me ?'

'No—why should I? It is what I supposed. But you have not quite truly answered my question.'

Geneste hesitated.

'There are things,' he said, 'that a man doesn't readily tell, even to the woman he loves best and trusts most—not so much because they show him in a bad light as because they concern another woman.'

'Helen came to my room this morning and begged me to ask you to tell me what you and she had been saying to each other this morning. Does that meet your objection ?'

'Did she—really? The girl is extraordinary ; she is tremendous ; she is sublime. Yes; she said that I might tell you, or that she would tell you herself, but I did not think she meant it. Clare, I am a beast—an idiot ; or perhaps it would be more to the point to say that I am a man.'

'Yes,' she answered, with a melancholy

smile—and for the first time, applied to himself, he heard a faint intonation of scorn in
her voice ; 'men never seem to rise, after
all, to being much more than men. Well, tell
me.'

Then he told her the whole story from the
beginning of his attraction towards Helen
—the kiss, the revulsion, the compact of
friendship—all up to their strange talk of that
fatal morning.

'If I were as noble as she is,' said Clare,
'I should resolve never to see you again ;
then you would in time forget me, and you
would, of course, get to care for her, and you
would be very happy.'

'Do you think that is possible — after
having loved you ?' He laughed again,
almost as he had laughed to Helen. 'The
whole thing is whimsical ; it's ridiculous.'

'It is cruel !' exclaimed Clare bitterly.

'Ah, you don't seem to see what is so clear
to me, that just this wonderful magnanimity
and candour prove her utter incomprehension
of love—as we know it. Her feeling for me,
poor child !—and Heaven knows how un-

worthy I am of it!—is a poem, a dream—
much the sort of thing that makes a certain
type of Roman Catholic girl want to be a
nun ; it's not flesh and blood, and the wound
doesn't bleed. That's my consolation, and
that reconciles me to the position I've put
myself into, which would be humiliating
enough to one's self in the ordinary way.'

'Do you remember saying to me that
night, at The Grave, that Helen Cusack was
one of the women who would know the real
thing when it came along ?' she asked.

'Yes, I remember. Well, the conception
of me as a fatuous fool gets a further justification. Jove must have been in a curiously
ironic mood when he portioned out to me such
splendid chances of happiness,' he added,
after a pause.

'Why do you call it ironic ?'

'There's something of the Tantalus touch
about the business, don't you think ?' he said
bitterly. 'My confession has not raised me
in your estimation. I feel that in your whole
manner.'

'Perhaps. But I have wronged that poor

girl.   Besides,' she added impetuously, 'last
night has made me realize again how impossible it all is.'

'Clare, have mercy !'

'I have mercy—too much mercy on you.
But I can have none on myself.   The worst
part of the whole thing is, to know you as—
just a man !'

'Neither saint nor hero,' he interjected.
'Be it so.   I withdraw all pretensions to a
superhuman virtue.   Well, dear, beautiful,
magnificent woman—and I can only wish
that you were still more woman——'

'Oh, don't—don't say that !'

'Why not ?   It is true.   But I will say
nothing that you wish unsaid.   Finish your
sentence.'

'Not now.   Those words take the sap out
of it.'

'I insist.   Go on.   The worst part of the
whole thing is,' he repeated, 'to know me
as just a man, and——   Go on.'

'And to love you because you are yourself !' she exclaimed.   'Just yourself—no
better than I am ; not so strong as even

Ambrose Blanchard showed himself to Gladys Hilditch.'

'You don't know the story of Ambrose Blanchard and Gladys Hilditch.'

' I can guess it. He left her——'

' For the reason that he did not love her as well as I love you.'

She made a gesture full of perplexity and pain.

' Well, if Ambrose did show superhuman virtue—putting your construction on the matter,' he went on, ' he may have his reward now. The next month or two will show whether he chooses to claim it. But don't let us talk of Blanchard and Mrs. Hilditch; let us talk of ourselves. Do you know, my dearest, a moment ago I was wretched at the idea of having made you despise me. Now I am almost glad to have fallen from my pedestal—glad since I heard those last words of yours. Down on earth, I'm nearer to you, in one sense, anyhow, and, as somebody said somewhere, pedestals are not comfortable places.'

' Dr. Geneste,' she said, looking at him

with great earnestness, 'I am quite serious in what I am going to ask you.'

'Mrs. Tregaskiss,' he rejoined, 'I promise to give your question my most serious attention.'

'Don't jest. I am too wretched to make jokes.'

His whole manner changed.

'Clare, my dearest, don't you know that I am ridiculously, boyishly happy? And do you know why? Because you said that you loved me—loved me because I am just my own imperfect self—not a saint nor a hero. I'm so delighted to get rid of my halo; it will become you far better. I'll put you on the pedestal now. I'll fall down and worship you; you need not be afraid that I shall fail in one iota of respect for you. Only why keep up the farce of conventionalities when there's no part to play and we are out of earshot of every living creature? You have not once called me by my name. Say it, Clare. I want to hear how it sounds from your lips.'

'What is it?' she asked perversely. 'Yes,

I know. Guy—Guy Geneste—Guy Living-
stone. Guy—what was the good heir of
Redclyffe called ?—Guy ! I don't like it ; it's
only fit for a novel or the theatre. That's
just it—what I hate—what makes me hate
myself. Good women don't play parts ; and
it's true, as you said, we have a part to
play ; but for goodness' sake let us keep
a spice of originality. We needn't repeat
the hackneyed business, " Call me Edwin,
dearest !" '

'Who is making jokes now ?'

She turned her head away ; he had known
that it was to hide her quivering lips even
when she spoke so lightly. Now she looked
at him full, and there was a scared expression
in her eyes.

'I'm in deadly earnest ; it has all come
over me—I've been feeling it these weeks
back. But last night, and in the dawn this
morning, after the fire, when I lay awake in
the overseer's house, with baby beside me,
and Ning and he were resting on the floor
near me, I felt that I was a wicked woman—
that I couldn't hold up my head and look

straight into the light of day. I felt that way
when Helen Cusack came into my room this
morning ; and I knew that she had found me
out, and that she was having a battle with
herself so that she mightn't seem to be
shrinking back from me. I felt that I must
end it all ; that last night must never come
again—it was the breaking of my vow. And
that's what I mean. I am going to ask you
never to come and see me at Mount Wombo
again. Go to Brinda Plains instead, and see
Helen Cusack. You can make some excuse
—you can get up a quarrel with my husband ;
that would be the best way.'

'Clare, you don't really mean this ; and,
if you do, can you imagine that it would be
possible for either of us ?'

'Everything is possible when one deter-
mines that it shall be so. You could marry
Helen Cusack, and I could bear to see you
her husband, if we had both made up our
minds to it.'

'Put that notion out of your head entirely,'
he said, with anger. 'Perhaps you would
have me take that poor quixotic child at

her word, and lay up a lifetime of misery for
her as well as for myself—and for you. Do
you think you would be any happier if you
condemned me to be miserable ?'

'I think,' she answered slowly, 'that we
are condemning each other every time we
meet to a worse misery than we could have
any other way.'

'Clare,' he said reproachfully, 'you have
made me happier than I have ever been in
all my life; and I had hoped that I was
helping you a little. You said so in the
beginning.'

'Ah! in the beginning. But we don't
seem able to keep at the beginning. It's all
a mistake,' she went on. 'We thought that
we were going to help each other—that we
were going to make a new world for each
other—that all the hard things were to become
easier and all the bad people better because
we loved each other.'

'And isn't it so ?' he asked tenderly.
'The world is much better to me because of
your love.'

'You think so just now that we are

together and alone.   But did you not confess
yesterday evening when we were walking in
the garden that it was torture to be with me
before other people—and wretchedness when
we were apart?'

'Yes, that is true.   But sometimes we are
alone together, and five minutes of such
happiness is worth a good deal of pain.'

'And yet,' she went on, 'when we are
alone together you are often tormented by—
by the limitations which, oh, Heaven! are
so easily overstepped.'

'You have said it,' he answered.   'I am
but human.   And I love you!'

'Oh, it is a mistake, a terrible mistake!'
she cried passionately.   'Our fine theories
and our raptures and all our resolves were
only a sort of glamour to cover up the lie.
That is what it is; that is what the world
has changed to—a lie! I am a lie to the
neighbours, to myself, to my children, and
to my husband.   What does it matter
whether he is bad or good? He is my
husband, and till I knew you I was true to
him in every action of my life, even if I were

false in the thoughts of my heart. Now I am false in heart and action, too. I am false when I lie down, false when I rise up, false when I hear my little child say her prayers, and she repeats after me, "God bless father and mother!" Guy, you are free; you have no other claims; you can live your life alone. But have you ever thought what it must mean to me—to go to sleep with one man's name on my lips, a name that is not my husband's—the thought of one man only in my heart, and the longing that we may be together in my dreams? Then to awaken with that one image in my mind, my dearest hope that you may come, or that I may have some word from you that day; to know that all my being is absorbed in you, and to know, too, that I am the wife of another man, who is the father of my children; to be living under that man's roof, eating his bread, wearing the clothes his money has bought me—never apart from him day nor night!'

The words rushed out. She did not look at Geneste as she said them, and, when she broke off, gave her horse a touch with the whip, and they cantered on for some time in silence. When they pulled up, he said very quietly :

'If you feel it so badly as that, my poor Clare, there are only two courses for us to choose between.'

'Two ?' she repeated feverishly.

'I must do what you say you wish—keep apart from you altogether. The best plan would be for me to go away, as I have sometimes thought I might.'

'Right away ?'

'Yes ; sell Darra-Darra, and go Home and pick up my old life again.'

He watched her face with an eagerness that was almost cruel, hoping that his words would wound her. He was satisfied. She gave an involuntary murmur of pain.

'Right away ?' she repeated. 'Back to England ! And I should stay out here, alone on the Leura—desolate !'

'It is the only way, if I am to obey your wish. I cannot remain at Darra, within thirty miles of you, and not come to see you. It would be beyond my power.'

She made a heroic effort.

'Very well. I think you are right. Go! The other would certainly be difficult for a man—who is just a man. Yes, you must go back to England.'

They were both silent for a minute or two, riding on under the gidia-trees. This noonday stillness seemed awful. Presently he said :

'I told you that there were two courses. You have never thought of the alternative ?'

'No.'

'It is a very simple one. I consider it a perfectly righteous one, according to all natural law. Many others of the world's thinkers—far better and wiser people than I —advocate it. Why should your whole life and mine be sacrificed to a mere chimæra invented by man ? The only real marriage is that of hearts and souls. Why should we be apart ? Why should you remain here desolate ? Why should you not come to England with me and be my dearly cherished wife and companion as long as our lives last ?'

She drew a deep breath, which was like a gasp.

'Because it is impossible,' she answered. 'How could I be your wife ?'

'Tregaskiss would be only too ready to take his freedom. There would be a divorce, and we should marry.'

Again there was a silence. Then she said abruptly :

'And my children ?'

'They are his children. You have often said that you did not love your children as you ought, because they were his.'

'I brought them into the world. I gave them life. Poor little things ! And they are girls, and will grow up to be women— perhaps women like their mother. And they will have no mother to help them to make a better thing of their life than she has done.'

'You had no mother.'

'If mine had lived, I might not have married Keith Tregaskiss.'

The dogs following behind started a kangaroo, and Clare's horse, which was fresh, snorted and tried to follow. After a minute or two it quieted down again.

'Clare,' Geneste said, ' I'm not going to talk heroics, or the kind of sentiment which, in plays, anyhow, goes with the proposal I've made. I only want you to know that I meant it, and that my life is yours as long as it or your own lasts. If it is to be a question between me and the children, just look at the matter this way, too. When your children are grown up they will leave you. Their interests will be apart from yours, and you will be desolate indeed. Your children are your fetters. Well, in nine or ten years, when you are still comparatively a young woman, Nature will release you from them — unless you go on forging new fetters, as you may do.'

He spoke deliberately.

She gave a shudder.

' It would be sacrificing a lifetime for a very few years. How shall you feel when those years are over, if you send me away now ? Of course, there is a chance of freedom coming in a different way.'

'Don't !' she interrupted hastily. 'Don't speak of that. I am not so bad as to specu-late on death or wrong-doing.'

'Well, I won't say any more ; and there is the Carmodys' fence. We needn't talk of it: only let the idea dwell in your mind, and shape itself—as a possibility.'

'No, no!' she cried. 'You must not even think of such a possibility. It is not a possibility; it is absolutely out of the question.'

'Do you wish me, then, to go away? I will obey you, if you command it.'

'Not yet. Let us give ourselves a chance of becoming sensible.' She smiled a miser-able smile, which contradicted the suggestion. 'Do what I ask you. Keep away from me —at least, for a time.'

'Very well. I will try to do so. I cannot promise you that I shall succeed.'

He got off his horse as he spoke, to let down the slip-rails of the Carmodys' paddock fence. She passed through, and then he put them up again, and they cantered towards the head-station.

Ballandean, as the place was called, looked ill-conditioned and poverty-stricken; and it was easy to see that as few hands as possible were employed in its working. The fences were out of repair, the lower part of the garden a wilderness, and the trees, which had been 'rung,' and some of which were felled, had been left still to cumber the ground. The gidia scrub which surrounded it added to its melancholy appearance. The house, like most station houses, stood upon a slight rise, at the foot of which was a creek, broadening here into several stagnant lily-grown lagoons. The entrance was at the back.

It had been a 'killing morning.' A flock of crows and hawks was hanging about the stockyard, not far off, and making swoops down towards the meat-store veranda, where Mr. Carmody, with his shirt-sleeves tucked up, was salting meat, assisted by a couple of black-boys. A tall, prematurely-aged girl, of eleven or twelve, had just taken away a tin dishful of unappetising morsels to fry for breakfast, which was very late that day; some other children were playing about the yard, and several black gins were squatted on their hams, nursing pickaninnies and smoking clay pipes—the reward for assistance in carrying down the 'cut-up' beast, and there were sundry dogs, of the kangaroo and a sort of pariah breed, sniffing round.

Mr. Carmody came forward, pulling down his shirt-sleeves, and greeting them with subdued geniality. He was a long, thin, disjointed-looking Bushman, weather-beaten, unkempt, and with a worried expression. He apologized to Mrs. Tregaskiss. She knew what 'killing' morning meant when there weren't many hands going. He and the black-boys had to do the salting between them; but it was pretty near finished, and he'd go up and get the cows milked, so as to have some fresh milk for breakfast. 'Only two of 'em, Mrs. Tregaskiss; this drought is drying up all the milkers.'

'You get on,' said Geneste, 'and finish up your salting. I'll go and milk the cows.

We've come upon you unawares, but I'm taking Mrs. Tregaskiss over to Darra; her husband is with the buggy, and is going by the short-cut, and we both thought it was a good chance of seeing Mrs. Carmody.'

'Well, I'm glad you've come, doctor, though we laughed at your doctoring last time you were over. The missus isn't just the thing. First time since I don't know when. Said she felt lazy this morning, and she hasn't got up yet.'

Geneste looked grave.

'How has Mrs. Carmody been feeling?' he asked.

'Well, I don't rightly know. Says there's a sort of numbness down one side of her, and that she could not swallow properly. And she's been having that stupid little cough a good deal and the pain in her chest.'

Geneste's face became graver still.

'You'll let me have a look at her to-day and see what that pain in her chest means,' he said.

'That's what I want, doctor. I don't believe it's anything, for it goes and she's all

right again.   Why, she says herself, if it
wasn't for pain and the sort of chokiness
she'd be the strongest and cheerfullest woman
on the Leura.   Cheerfullest she is, anyhow,'
added Mr. Carmody with his perplexed little
laugh; 'and it isn't a bit like her to give
in, though it is only once in a way, and there
can't be much amiss, for she was laughing
like anything a bit ago.   But I think I'd just
like you to go in and see her before you
start again.'

'Certainly !   Shall I go now, or milk the
cow first ?'

'Well—if you didn't mind—the missus
always has her glass of fresh milk and a
dash of rum and egg about ten or eleven
o'clock ; and we're awfully behind this morning.   Mrs. Tregaskiss, don't you bother about
that pack'—as Clare was unfastening the pack-
ages from the dees of her saddle.   'Things
for my wife is it ?   Well, that's really kind
of Mrs. Cusack.   Hi ! Black Billy there,
you take it yarraman belonging Mrs. Tregaskiss.   And how's all at Brinda ?'

'I suppose you don't know that we were

all burnt out last night?' said Clare; and then, amid many ejaculations on the part of Mr. Carmody and of the child with the dish of meat, who had stopped to listen, she told the story, Geneste in the meanwhile un-saddling and leading the horses to the yard, and then going to the milkers. Mr. Car-mody, wiping the salt from his hands, led Mrs. Tregaskiss into a roughly-furnished sitting-room, which had somehow a forlorn look as if the mistress had not put things straight that morning, the kerosene lamp un-trimmed and with a black rim round its bowl, made of dead flying ants and moths, and Mrs. Carmody's basket of mendings on the sewing machine stand, a half-darned sock hanging out of it.

'We're in a dreadful muck this morning,' said Mr. Carmody. 'The missus does the tidying—always up first and doing her lamps and cleaning round. Ah! Mrs. Tregaskiss, when I see her at it and think of what she was when I married her—one of the prettiest girls down Sydney way, and used to gaiety and comforts and English ways like the best of them ; not but what you are an example of that too—I say to myself that a man has no right to bring a woman out West unless he's a Company's manager like Cusack, or a millionaire like Cyrus Chance.'

Clare, following Geneste's lead, put the room tidy and talked to the children, while Carmody went in to prepare his wife for her visitor.

By-and-by he came out and told Clare she might go in and she'd find Mrs. Carmody quite herself and wanting to get up and see after things, but she—Mrs. Tregaskiss—mustn't let her. And he scurried off, enjoining the eldest girl to hurry up in the kitchen.

'Come in, Mrs. Tregaskiss,' said a faint voice, as Clare knocked at the door.

Mrs. Carmody's room looked more dainty and comfortable than the rest of the house, though the floor was only of earth, covered with skins and rugs, and it had no glass windows, only wooden shutters. But there were pictures hanging on the canvas walls ; and the dressing-table was covered with chintz, and there were some cushioned squatters' chairs and a writing-table. Mrs. Carmody was lying, supported by pillows, in the big bed, with the mosquito curtains drawn up, their pink glazed calico bows dangling at the head and making spots of colour, which matched the spots on Mrs. Carmody's cheek, deepened now by the exertion of getting into a fresh frilled nightgown in honour of her visitor.

There was to Clare something intensely pathetic in this effort of the dying woman to be equal to the occasion. For she was dying. There could be no doubt of that; and for a moment Mrs. Tregaskiss' heart stood still in the shock of dismay. But the little pretty thing, who, though she was thirty-five, looked extraordinarily girlish and charming with her fluffy yellow hair, bright eyes, and spiritualized expression, laughed on.

'It's quite absurd for me to be in bed. But this morning I really felt so tired that I said to Jem I thought I would take it easy a bit, and have the little ones in with me and

amuse them, while Jennie was doing my
work.   Jem says I'd better see Dr. Geneste,
as he has come over ; but I can't tell the use.
For there's nothing the matter, except just
that I feel queer and numblike, and this
troublesome pain in my chest, that comes
and goes, and seems to choke me for the
moment.'   Clare noticed that her voice
changed oddly as she talked ; and then her
cough hindered her utterance, and she leaned
back and gulped as though she were being
strangled.   The attack went off in a minute
or two, and she gasped, with a smile ·
' There, it's gone now !   I am all right
again.   I dare say Dr. Geneste will tell me
of something for it, and I shall be quite well
to-morrow.'

' I think you had better see him, dear Mrs.
Carmody,' said Clare, afraid lest her choked
voice might betray her, for she felt extremely
anxious.

'Oh, well, I will, then, after you have had
luncheon and they've brought me my own
" doctor," as I call my twelve o'clock rum-and-
milk.   Are your cows drying up, and dying,

too, with the drought, Mrs. Tregaskiss ? It's
quite dreadful with us ; we can hardly get
enough for the babies. Jem says those dreadful Unionists have burned down the house and
wool-shed at Brinda Plains ; you don't mean
to say it's true ! Now tell me all about it.'

And Clare told her, and sat beside her and
listened to her chatter, and assented to her
cheerful protestations that there was nothing
much the matter, and praised the looks of the
younger children, who were playing about the
room, till at last Mr. Carmody, in a clean
shirt and a coat, his hands cleansed from salt
and brine, pushed open the door and cheerily
ushered in Dr. Geneste.

'All right, doctor, you can have your way
at last and overhaul the old lady—you've
been wanting it long enough, and we've
always laughed at you. And don't you go
telling us there's anything really amiss, for
that colour of hers will give you the lie, and
we shall laugh at you—the two of us—again.
You doctors — even when they're unpro-
fessional ones like you—are always hankering
after a case.'

CHAPTER XXIV.

POOR MRS. CARMODY!

THE doctor seemed to be a very long time with the sick woman. When he came out there was a look upon his face which Mrs. Tregaskiss had never before seen. It was strange how in a moment he had become an abstraction, removed from all personal stress and excitement; not the man, but the physician; a mere factor, as it were, of the mighty human tragedy beside which individual emotions sink into comparative nothingness. For Clare, too, the balance of things seemed to have been startlingly readjusted. Geneste the physician acquired a dignity that in their last interview had been wanting in Geneste the man. The new aspect of him had a curiously sobering effect upon her. She realized that her own sorrow was but as a drop in the ocean of human wretchedness. Her drama and his had become absorbed in and annihilated by the thrilling drama of death into which they had been suddenly thrown.

It was terrible to see Mr. Carmody's unconcern and absolute unconsciousness of the impending catastrophe. He had sat with Clare in the sitting-room waiting for the doctor, the breakfast-table spread, and talked about the Brinda Plains fire, the Unionists, the drought, Tregaskiss' Bores, never suspecting that his own fate and that of his dearest hung upon the examination going on within that closed door.

'Well, doctor,' he said cheerily, when Geneste appeared, 'is she going to get up? Have you given her a good scolding for her laziness? Eh—man! What—what is the matter?'

Geneste went straight to him.

'Carmody,' he said in a low voice, deeply moved, 'there's no good in blinking things—

to you, anyhow. I've got to break bad news.
You've heaps of pluck, old fellow, and you'll
want it. You've got to bear a shock—the
worst a man can have to bear.'

'Eh!—what—what do you mean?' stammered Carmody, frightened and taken aback
by Geneste's manner.

'Your wife is very ill indeed—very, very
ill. Do you understand?' Carmody was
staring stupidly. 'She has been bad for a
long time,' Geneste went on, 'and neither of
you have realized it. Now I am sorry to
have to tell you that there is no—that there
is very great danger.'

'Danger!' repeated Carmody, still blankly.

'Very great danger—imminent danger.'

'But what do you mean, man?' roared
Carmody. 'Why, she was laughing at me
a minute ago! Danger! You must be
dreaming; you don't know what you are
talking about.'

'I wish that I did not. Look here,
Carmody; I've got to make it clear to you.
I wish to God I could give you any hope, but
I can't.'

'Can't—give—me—any—hope!' repeated poor Carmody, with a jerk between each word, while he gazed fixedly at the doctor, as though he were fascinated by some horrible sight. Then, 'Will you please to tell me,' he cried almost angrily, 'what is the matter with my Bessy?'

'Your wife has an aortic aneurism,' replied Geneste. 'The pain in her chest, which I felt sure could not mean lung mischief, and the little choking cough, and other symptoms of which I have heard, have made me afraid of late months that it might be the case, though the disease is not common with women, especially when comparatively young. That is what made me hesitate to speak of my suspicion, and you wouldn't hear of my approaching Mrs. Carmody medically. Now, since I have examined her chest, and have felt the pulsating swelling, I have no doubt; and I don't know what to say to you or how to advise you about—about'—Geneste's own voice broke—'about conveying to her the fact that she may not have long to live.'

'Geneste! Doctor—you don't mean—you can't mean that she is dying?'

'I am afraid,' said Geneste, in a low, emphatic voice which shook with pity, 'that I must tell you what is the truth. She may die at any moment. She may live a week— a fortnight; she may die within the next half-hour.'

Carmody burst into a hysterical laugh.

'Tell her she is dying! Do you expect me to believe it? You don't know your business, doctor; you're deceived — you're out of practice!'

'Do you think I'd say a thing like that to you if I wasn't sure? Go in, Carmody; look at her, talk to her, believe what I say. I know it's an awful blow. I'm only doing my duty in telling you straight. Go in—try to be calm. Talk to her. You know her, and you know what she would wish, and if she would choose to leave her children and you without a word.'

Mr. Carmody sank helplessly upon a chair.

'You want me to tell her—that she is

dying.   Tell her—my poor little Bessy ! who
was planning only last night how we'd take a
trip to Sydney when the bad times were over
and put Jennie to school.   My Bessy—the
pluckiest, cheeriest—tell her she is dying !
No ; I'm damned if I can do that.',

He broke down altogether, and, lurching
forward, his head on his arms, cried like a
child.

A voice came from the sick-room : 'Jem!'
The door was thin, and there were wide
canvas-covered gaps between the slabs on the
wall.   The poor woman must have heard
that despairing cry.   'What is it he says he
can't do ?' the feeble voice went on ; and just
then the two little children, who had run in
from the veranda to their mother as soon as
the doctor had left her, set up a wail.
Geneste looked at Clare.

'Will you go to her?   I will do what I can
with him, poor chap !'

Just then Jennie, the eldest girl, came in,
followed by a half-caste with a dish of smoking
fry.

'It's ready, father,' she said.   'Shall I take

some in to mother ?' And then she stood still, her gaze fixed in consternation upon her father, who was sobbing with his head on the luncheon-table. Clare took her hand.

'Jennie dear,' she whispered, 'come and take the children away. The doctor has been telling your father that your mother is very ill, and he wants to talk to her.'

'Oh, Mrs. Tregaskiss!'

The child's eyes grew rounder, but she said no more. She was a wise little creature, and went in with Clare to her mother's room and took out the babies, who were fighting with each other and crying on the floor.

Mrs. Carmody was half sitting up in bed. Something of that look which nurses call 'the change' had come into her face; the laugh had gone, and the smile had given place to an expression of terror.

'Take them away, Jennie—out into the veranda; perhaps I shall want them pre-sently. Mrs. Tregaskiss,' she gasped, 'tell me—what is it? What has the doctor been saying to Jem? Has he been telling him that I shall never get any better? Tell me;

you needn't be afraid.   I heard him say the
word—dying ; and I saw it in his face.   Am
I dying ?'

Clare's only answer was to take the poor
thing in her arms and to put the wan face,
with the pink all gone out of it now, against
her own.

' I feel so strange,' said Mrs. Carmody ; ' it
came on a little while ago.   Lay me down
again.'

She was perfectly calm.   After a few
minutes, she said :

' Poor Jem !   That was him crying.   I am
so glad I've been a comfort to him.'

There was a little pause filled by Clare in
arranging the poor thing more comfortably
on her pile of pillows.   There were no
medicines ; there was nothing to give her ;
it seemed so unlike most sick-rooms when
the sick person is in extremity.

' Mrs. Tregaskiss,' Mrs. Carmody began
again.   The big bright eyes searched Clare's
face through and through, with, as Clare
thought later, that sort of prescience which
comes sometimes to the dying.   ' Listen ; I

want to say something to you. Once I was
nearly leaving Jem and the babies, and going
off with another man, because I loved him
and he was rich and I hated the Bush. But
I didn't; and I am so thankful now I'm
dying that I didn't. Do you know, it's the
first thought that seems to come to me. Oh,
it's such a comfort, when you are dying, to
know that you've managed to keep straight,
and that you've looked after the children the
best way you could.'

Clare went out. The words were like
insistent hands knocking at her heart. Poor
Mr. Carmody met her, groping his way, it
seemed, his eyes nearly blinded with crying.
He went in and closed the door. Clare
heard a plaintive call, ' Jem!' and then a
stifled murmur, as the husband and wife held
their last talk together.

Geneste was sitting in the parlour, waiting
till he should be wanted again. There was
something terribly grim in the look of the
spread table, the untasted luncheon, and the
dish of fry getting cold and soddened, with
the fat hardening into round white spots on

the gravy. Clare exchanged a few hurried words with Geneste about Mrs. Carmody's condition, and he confirmed her fear that the end was very close. His solicitude on her own behalf jarred inexpressibly upon Clare. She waved away with impatience his entreaty that she would eat something, or at least have a drink of the fresh milk from which Mrs. Carmody's 'doctor' had been taken.

'No, no!' she cried almost angrily. 'How can I eat? How can I think of anything but——'

'But——' She hurried away from him. What she was thinking of was that speech of Mrs. Carmody's: 'It's such a comfort when you're dying to know that you've managed to keep straight, and that you've looked after the children the best way you could.'

In the veranda Jennie was nursing the youngest child. She was crying softly, her tears falling on its hair, while the two next smallest were whining and squabbling at her knee.

'Oh, hush! Jake and Kathleen—hush!' cried poor Jennie. 'I can't tell you a story.

They want me to tell them a story, Mrs. Tregaskiss. Mother was telling them stories when——' And Jennie's tears fell.

' Mother's stories are beautiful,' said Jake ; ' all about the people who lived with gods and goddesses, and got changed into things.'

' I will tell you a story, then,' said Clare, ' about someone who lived with the gods and goddesses, and whom a wicked goddess tried to change into a pig. It's the story of a king who went sailing and sailing, and got into strange countries and among very curious people.'

' Oh, I know that,' put in Jake contemptuously. ' It's only " Sinbad and the Old Man of the Sea." There are no gods in that.'

' You don't know my story. It wasn't Sinbad ; it was a king, very brave and wise, who went a long, long way from his wife and his son to fight for his friend. And when the war was over, after many years, Ulysses —that was the king's name—took his ships and started to go home. Well, on his way back there was a storm, and the ships were brought to a land where there lived a very wicked and beautiful woman. She sat spinning in her palace a web of the most brilliant colours, and watching for some man to come along, that she might pretend to love him and give him to drink of her cup of witches' wine, in which she had mixed all kinds of dreadful herbs and enchantments, so that when he had drunk it he would forget everything, and she would have the power to change him into some horrible beast.'

'That's a good story,' put in Jake appreciatively.

'And outside her palace were wild beasts watching, too, while she wove her web. There was a leopard——'

The bedroom door opened with a sharp click, and Mr. Carmody came out. He made a sign to Dr. Geneste to go in, and then called quietly to Jennie and the little ones. He told Jennie to go and find her brothers and bring them, because their mother wanted to speak to them all; and then, taking the two little ones by the hand, bade them be

very good and listen attentively to what
mother said.

Clare waited in the veranda. Afterwards
Geneste told her how it had been. How
Mrs. Carmody had kissed each of them, and
had told each separately to try and be good
and to love the others; and that, though she
was going out of their sight, she should
always be near, watching to see if they
obeyed her, and that it would make ' Mother '
very glad and happy to know that they were
good; she bade Jennie in especial take care
of her father and the little ones; and she
bade the boys to tell the truth always, and to
follow their father in all things. Then, just
as she was trying to lift herself, that she
might kiss the baby again, she fell back, and
when they looked at her she was dead.

Geneste rode on to Darra, before he went
sending one of the Ballandean black-boys
to Brinda Plains with a note to Mrs. Cusack,
telling her what had happened, and begging
her to find means of communication with the
clergyman at Ilganda. He felt sure that kind
Mrs. Cusack, in spite of her own worries

after the fire, would come over to the desolate
children, or would, at least, send the wife of
the store-keeper, or one of the women from
the Workings. He did not spare his horse,
and was back again that night, to find that
his anticipations were justified: Mrs. Cusack
was there, and had taken the command of
everything.

It needed just such an energetic, practical
person, with abundance of the milk of human
kindness for those in need, to rouse the
bereaved husband, stupefied with the shock
of his sudden calamity. Mrs. Cusack made
all the arrangements, got black stuff from the
store, and, with the help of Mrs. Tregaskiss
and the overseer's wife, rigged out the poor
children in mourning. The clergyman from
Ilganda arrived shortly; he was not a resident
there, but was doing his half-yearly official
duty in the way of baptisms and marriages.

On the third day Mrs. Carmody was
buried under a clump of gum-trees by the
creek, on the knoll above flood-mark. One
of her babies, who had died a few days after
its birth, was buried there—it was after that

last baby's coming that she had begun to get
thin and to have her worrying little cough
and pain—and the place had been a favourite
walk of the poor lady's, when her day's work
was over.   She had been used to sit there in
the cool of the evening with her sewing and
tell the children stories.   The funeral was
very quiet and very pathetic ; the overseer's
wife and Mrs. Cusack wept bitterly.

Clare Tregaskiss did not cry, but her heart
was like lead ; and once Geneste, who was
there, caught a wild, strange look which she
cast out into the gidia forest, and wondered
of what she was thinking.   She had not
allowed him opportunity for a single word of
private conversation.   He was then even
more unhappy than she was.   He wrote her
a long letter, which he got conveyed to her,
begging her to forgive him for his proposal,
if he had shocked or affronted her, repeating
his arguments in sober, matter-of-fact fashion,
asseverating his unalterable devotion, and,
in conclusion, promising that he would obey
whatever command she chose to put upon
him.   Her answer was four words only,

scribbled upon a piece of paper, which she herself put into his hand after the funeral—
'Keep away from me.'

Helen Cusack did not come to the funeral, but sent a beautiful cross of white lilies and maidenhair fern; Tottie and Minnie and Miss Lawford sent one also, and there were many humbler tributes on the coffin, perhaps the most touching of all the nosegays of native jasmine, thrown by Jake and Kathleen, in gathering which Clare had kept them quiet the whole of the previous afternoon.

It was a sad little family tragedy, but not uncommon in the outside districts, where delicate ladies lead the lives of peasant women, in a tropical climate, with the enfeebling influence of heat, which, at least, the peasant woman of the Northern Hemisphere has not to contend with. The strong grow patient, resourceful, and hardy; the weak become patient and resourceful, too, but after a time fall and do not get up again. The stockmen's wives and the working women, inheriting a strain of endurance in their blood, get on in the out-country fairly well, and live to see their children's children ; but the refined, fragile ladies will do the work of six slaveys, bear their hardships and their children without a murmur, and fight drought, heat, blight, and fever with indomitable courage for a few years, then all of a sudden will develop rapid consumption or some other insidious disease, and die just as their children are getting out of babyhood and the pleasant afternoon of life is coming on them.

Clare Tregaskiss was immensely affected by the melancholy incident. It seemed to her a foreshowing of her own fate. It would not be consumption that she would develop, but heart disease, like Mrs. Carmody. Geneste had warned her. And then where would have been the use of renunciation ? Her little daughters would be as utterly bereft as though she had basely forsaken them for the sake of her own selfish joy. And what good would Keith get from her sacrifice ?—what good in any case, since he had already discovered that she was incapable

of making him happy? Where was the use
of any effort towards living straight in this
universal crookedness? Where was the use
of poor Helen's romantic love for Geneste;
of her own ten years' struggle to meet her
fate stoically and to conform herself to her
life? What was the good of having kept all
these years a calm face and a heart unstirred
in its depths if she were to succumb like an
undisciplined schoolgirl, her passion and her
pain only intensified by the years of re-
pression? Yet those words of Mrs. Carmody's
haunted her, and filled her alternately with a
sense of remorseful guilt and of immense and
angry revolt. Should she when she was
dying rejoice that she had 'managed to keep
straight'? Rather, might not the same
ghastly doubt which had occurred to her at
Mrs. Carmody's bedside embitter her own
death-throes?—the doubt that perhaps, if that
other woman had not kept straight, poor
soul! but had gone the way of frail woman-
hood, she would have had, at any rate, her
hour of blessedness, and almost certainly a
longer time afterwards in which to repent

than had been allotted to her for the doing of her prosaic duty.

The Darra-Darra plan was upset, or, rather, postponed, by this untoward event. Geneste's Ballandean messenger had met the buggies from Brinda Plains striking off for the short-cut, and on learning what had occurred, Helen Cusack decided on her own responsibility to turn back, taking Miss Lawford and the children with her. She knew that her mother would certainly go to Ballandean, and guessed that Geneste would remain for the funeral, and that, on the whole, visiting Darra was inexpedient just then. Perhaps Tregaskiss' surly mood was accounted for by this change of programme. He had gone on with Gladys Hilditch, and when Geneste arrived had expressed himself extremely dissatisfied at his wife's non-appearance. Clare knew quite well how his mood had worked. He had grumbled that he wanted her back at Mount Wombo, and that he wished to get there himself as soon as possible ; there was no knowing what the Unionists might be up to ; and now that

poor Mrs. Carmody was dead and done for,
it wasn't as if she—Clare—could do any good
by staying at Ballandean. At any rate, he
meant to go on home the next day, and she
might do as she pleased. This was the
message sent.

Geneste had said that he should be delighted to escort Mrs. Tregaskiss straight
over to Mount Wombo from Ballandean;
they could easily manage it by changing
horses at Darra.

'Oh, you may escort her to the devil, if
you like!' roared Tregaskiss. 'I don't want
to interfere with you.'

He pulled himself up a moment later and
blurted out a sort of apology: 'The sun had
given him an infernal headache; he didn't
know what he was saying.' Geneste saw
that he had been 'nipping'—the Leura
euphemism—and turned away in silent and
contemptuous acceptance of the apology.
Gladys Hilditch, who was sitting in the
veranda, raised her eyebrows and went on
with her book, pretending she had heard
nothing. Yet Gladys was sorry for poor

Tregaskiss. She divined, if Geneste did not, something of the conflict of elemental emotions which was waging within him; it was not Tregaskiss' way to keep his thoughts and feelings to himself, and on the road over he had opened out a little to Gladys. She knew that wounded pride, lawless attraction, jealousy, a galling sense of inferiority and of wrong-doing, paternal affection and conjugal impulse—all the wilder and all the softer influences—were contending in that rude breast; and she fancied, correctly enough, that if Clare were to appeal to him in this mood, were to take him cleverly—if, indeed, it were worth while that she should do so; for, ah! was it worth while? Gladys asked herself—she might discover that Keith's infatuation for Miss Lawford, as well as his evil tempers, were all part of a perverted longing for sympathy and of a perverted love for herself.

Tregaskiss caught up Ning, hugging her with savage boisterousness.

'That's my Pickaninny! We two are going to stick together, anyhow, aren't we,

Pickaninny? Mummy can go her own way; it's Dad that Ningie holds on by. She's a fine plucky one, this Pickaninny, and Daddy will teach her to beat them all on horseback before she's six months older.'

'Daddy,' said Ning, seizing her opportunity, 'Mummy wouldn't let me ride to Brinda; and Mummy says I mustn't go, when we have the picnic, to Lake Eungella. Mummy says that wild blacks sit down along-a Eungella, and that mumkull (kill) Ningie. Mine think it Mummy says that because she no want Ningie to go. Poor Ning!' And the child put on her appealing face. 'Plenty that fellow want to go Lake Eungella.'

Tregaskiss burst into his loud laugh.

'Right you are, Ningie. Mummy's been gammoning you. Oh, there's no taking in this Pickaninny!'

'Ning no frightened of Myall Blacks,' protested the child, encouraged by her father's laugh. 'That *is* all gammon, isn't it, Daddy? My believe no blacks, only fairies, and princes, and nice story-people, sit down there. Daddy said so. Promise—please, Daddy,

promise that Ning shall ride to Lake Eungella.'

'All right, by Jove! Daddy promises.
Ning shall ride to Lake Eungella, whether
Mummy agrees or not—though,' he added,
'there isn't much prospect of that picnic
coming off yet awhile, I fancy.'

'Ning,' said Mrs. Hilditch later, 'you are
your father's child.'

'Yes,' averred Ning placidly, 'I Daddy's
Pickaninny.'

'Ning, you are a humbug; you are a
time-server; you are a traitress. And listen
to this—we are not going to Lake Eungella.'

Whereupon Ning was silent, and for
several minutes ruminated. Presently she
looked up.

'Auntie Gladys '—that was what she had
been told to call Mrs. Hilditch—'mine want
to ask you something. Plenty mine try to
find out.'

'Well, what is it, Pickaninny?'

'Auntie Gladys, suppose Ningie go bong
—I mean suppose Ningie die—will there be
any yarraman for me to ride in heaven, or

only those two fellow horses that took up Elijah's buggy?'

This was Ning's fashion of diverting attention from an embarrassing subject.

Gladys threw down her book with a peal of laughter.

'Ning, you are an imp—a demon! Go and ask your father.'

As it happened, Mrs. Tregaskiss did not take that long ride under Geneste's escort— did not, indeed, go back with him at all to Mount Wombo.

Gladys Hilditch begged permission to remain at Darra, instead of accompanying Tregaskiss and the children, and after the funeral the party from Ballandean — the clergyman and another of the mourning guests rode with them thus far—found her there, and also Cyrus Chance, whose aid Gladys had by some means convoked. Old Cyrus took both his 'Fair Ines' and the Mistress to Mount Wombo on the morrow, Geneste remaining at Darra.

'You see that I begin to obey you,' he whispered to Clare as they parted.

LIBRARY UNIVERSITY OF ILLINOIS

Mrs. Tregaskiss could not imagine how it was that Cyrus Chance, who never visited a neighbour except on strict business, should on this occasion have taken it into his head to pay a friendly call at Darra. Gladys might have enlightened her, and so might a certain black-boy of the camp where Mrs. Hilditch had been amusing herself for an hour or two the day before. The black-boy bought a new set of moleskins and a red flannel shirt, and got well drunk on the strength of 'that budgery fellow White Mary's' liberality.

CHAPTER XXV.

THE BABES FORBID.

THE great fire at Brinda Plains, in which both the head-station and the wool-shed, with all the bales of wool ready for carting southwards, had been destroyed, created an immense commotion in the district. It had been very cleverly done, so the authorities agreed, and there was a good deal of furtive pleasantry at the expense of Mr. Cusack and the Specials. The two harmless-looking diggers, who had halted to give the news of the dispersion of the Unionist force, had, no doubt, themselves been Unionists in disguise, and had imposed upon the police by the very staleness of their trick, too obvious to be suspected as a trick.

Of course they had taken advantage of
the relaxation of discipline in the watching,
and of the roistering that evening at the
Bachelors' Quarters—which had inclined the
Specials and gentlemen defenders to a sleep
heavier than usual—in order to steal, under
cover of the moonless night, round the head-
station, and fire it in the two most convenient
places.   Then, when all hands were engaged
in struggling with that conflagration, the
incendiaries had completed their business by
starting a second at the wool-shed, and had
then made away into safe hiding as speedily
as they could.

For three weeks and more, after poor Mrs.
Carmody's sudden death, nothing was heard
in the district but rumours of warlike opera-
tions, of pursual, discovery, and arrest, most
of which rumours were, unfortunately, not
corroborated.   The police scoured the country
in all directions, the squatters turned out to
assist them, and a fresh force of Specials
was enrolled and sent up.   The Specials
were, in those days, quite a feature of the
neighbourhood.   They did not spend all the

time in the saddle ; there were off-days, and
days and nights of watching at stations, so
that the smart gray uniform was to be seen
at many a dinner-table and at many an
impromptu dance, while the gray felt hats,
picturesquely turned up at one side, became
pretty generally adorned with the black and
red crest feather of the black cockatoo, which
it was the fashion for the Leura young ladies
to present to their gallant defenders, whom,
however, fate perversely defrauded of any
opportunity of proving their valour on the
battlefield.

For the Unionists skulked and would not
fight. Kelso, their leader, knew the district
better than either squatters or soldiers, with
the exception, perhaps, of Geneste, and led
the pursuing enemy a devious dance along
dry watercourses, through country which
that invincible enemy, thirst, at last com-
pelled them to evacuate. It was to Geneste
that the glory of capturing Kelso fell. The
old lion in him roused itself, and the explorer
did a ride and led a piece of tracking said to
be unparalleled in the Australian record of

criminal hunts.   Then there was a short,
sharp tussle with desperate men, shots were
fired, one of their number killed, and Geneste
himself slightly wounded.

Finally, Kelso and one or two others of
the ringleaders were arrested, the mob
listened to terms formulated by a committee
of squatters, and peace settled once more on
the Leura.

It was after Christmas that all this happened, and in the meantime Gladys Hilditch
had plenty of opportunity for acquiring information concerning the labour movement
in Australia.   But Gladys' interest in this,
and in the Bush generally, seemed to have
waned since the fire at Brinda Plains.   She
had grown very silent.   Latterly she had
spent a good deal of her time in dreamy
reverie.   Sometimes she was a little irritable,
and sometimes she looked sad.

There had been a week or two in which
she was almost perfectly happy—a sort of
afterglow following upon that divine moment
when she had awakened in the garden to
find herself lying upon Blanchard's arm, with

Blanchard's face bent over her in agonized tenderness, and passionate words of love pouring from his lips. He had called her ' Gladys — his dearest — his love !' had entreated her forgiveness, and, in the broken, incoherent sentences that it was bliss to hear, had wiped out the doubt, the pain, and the vain regret of those four years which had passed since Ironside's death put a tragic end to their intimacy. Then she had opened her eyes, and they had met his, and she knew that he must have read in them all that in her dazed condition she could not speak. The awakening had been so strange; she had fancied at first that it was a dream ; then she heard the shouts round her, the sound of falling timber, saw the red glare, realized that she was in her nightdress, the opossum rug round her, drenched with water, and had gone off into peals of hysterical laughter.

Mrs. Cusack had come to her, and they carried her into one of the outhouses, and by-and-by, Clare, agitated and hysterical, too, had helped her dress. By this time the head-station was a smouldering mass, and all the force of the place had collected at the workings in a futile attempt to save the wool-shed. Blanchard had gone with the rest, and she had never seen him since. The next day, when everything was over, and the Cusacks were mournfully taking stock of the ruins, she was told, just before the start to Darra, that he had hurt himself in trying to save some horses confined in a stable at the back of the wool-shed. The injury was nothing serious, Geneste had pronounced ; but he had ordered Blanchard to keep quiet, and the order remained in force till Tregaskiss and the Brinda Plains buggy had set off. Gladys had a bitter suspicion later that he had wished to avoid her, but it was not till the strike was ended, and there was nothing to hinder him from riding over to Mount Wombo, that she acknowledged to herself the suspicion.

In the excitement and scurrying about the country after the fire, personal drama seemed pretty much at a standstill. Tregaskiss went out with the Specials. His physical courage

was his best point, and it was probably to his
daring and animal vigour that he owed such
influence as he possessed over a certain type
of woman.   After the fire he was away from
home off and on for some time, Mr. Hansen
being recalled from the out-station, and, with
Shand, taking charge at Mount Wombo.

Station work was put aside everywhere
just now.   The district had not got over the
effects of the strike; the Cusack family was
occupied in mourning its losses and in making
plans for rebuilding, Mr. Cusack's anger ex-
pending itself in frenzied trips to the Ilganda
police-station, and in the direction of his
Free Labour men, whom he employed in
collecting building material.   Mrs. Cusack,
with her characteristic energy, set to work
remodelling the Bachelors' Quarters as a temporary residence, the young men having
established themselves in some of the stockmen's huts.

In all these weeks Geneste had rigorously
abstained from seeing Clare.   She heard of
his doings, of his part in the capture of
Kelso, of his accident, which, like most

casualties, gained in the repeating, and she
suffered untold agonies of anxiety and of
longing to see him and assure herself that
all was well. She had not expected that he
would accept her prohibition so literally ; she
had fancied that, at least, he would write,
that he would implore her to reconsider her
decision, that he would express regret for
that mad proposition of flight, and renew
his vows of Platonic friendship ; she hoped,
in spite of herself, that he would disobey
her—for he had made no definite promise—
and one day appear at Mount Wombo. He
did not write ; he did not come. The days
dragged on, and perhaps it was well for her,
and Gladys, too, that there was work to be
done, and that life was full just now of minor
privations. The mosquitoes swarmed ; milk
began to fail ; there was no butter. Even
the Chinaman found a difficulty in keeping
his garden watered and in producing the
melons and pumpkins which made dinner
not altogether an empty mockery. The
baby got a skin eruption, and was cross because of her first tooth ; and Gladys was

flagging in spirits, and did not now extol the picturesqueness of the Leura; no one came to Mount Wombo except the objectionable Mr. Micklethwaite, on his way back from that very droving trip which had brought him near Mrs. Tregaskiss at The Grave.

Clare made some whimsical reflections upon workings of coincidence and upon the law of causes in the spiritual region. But for that ill-bred speech of Micklethwaite's, she might never have betrayed her secret misery to Geneste; the hour would have passed, and he might, as even he had said the other day, be now Helen's promised husband. She was tormented in these weeks of apparent desertion by a jealousy of Helen, which she felt to be ignoble. She fancied that Geneste had ceased to love her, and that his errant fancy had returned to Helen. Poor woman! she found no comfort in despising him.

She had told herself that it was not likely he should think so much of her while the district was perturbed by the strikers. But now that scare was over; all the

squatters had settled down to their ordinary
avocations, and it might be supposed that
he, too, had resumed his former interests.
She did not suspect him of a deliberate
scheme to test his influence, based upon
scientific and philosophic observation of
woman's nature.

If this were so, he miscalculated his
strength, though it would be truer to as-
sume that he was actuated by motives less
unworthy than any such cold-blooded, selfish
design, and that he manfully struggled against
temptation ever present.

Even when temptation became opportunity, he struggled still. It presented itself
in the shape of a letter from Mrs. Cusack,
begging that she might now take advantage
of the proposal he had made just after the
fire and with which Mrs. Carmody's death
had interfered, and that he would receive the
two girls in the schoolroom, Helen and Miss
Lawford, for a week or ten days, while the
Bachelors' Quarters were being papered and
their rooms had to be vacated.

The suggestion that Mrs. Tregaskiss and

Mrs. Hilditch should be invited to Darra at the same time came as well from Mrs. Cusack, though on receipt of her letter the temptation had at once taken shape in his mind. Geneste had ridden over from Darra in answer to the letter, that he might give a warm personal endorsement to the invitation ; and they were seated after luncheon in the veranda of the Bachelors' Quarters, which commanded a now melancholy prospect of the back - garden and old entrance to the house, of which the new foundations were rising from the charred ruins.

'Ah !' sighed Mrs. Cusack, 'it upsets me to look at that. And just think of what my garden and the tennis-ground will be when those workmen have done trampling on them. Upon my word, I could cry for hours over our misfortune—though, of course, it's an alleviation that the Company bears part of the expense of rebuilding—if I didn't force myself to think of those poor Carmodys, and to remember that his loss, poor man ! is worse than mine. To be sure, if we hadn't been burned out they would have

been the gainers, for, of course, I'd have had
all the children over on a long visit—I hear
they're running quite wild—and Miss Lawford might have taken Jennie at lessons with
Tottie and Minnie.'

'There's room for her, too, at Darra-
Darra, Mrs. Cusack, if you like to arrange
it so,' said Geneste.

'Well, I don't know,' answered Mrs.
Cusack uneasily. 'I think I'd better not
begin, since one doesn't feel certain how
long it might last. The truth is, Dr. Geneste'
—and she looked round to assure herself that
the governess and the children were out of
earshot, at the same time casting a disap-
proving glance at Tregaskiss, who, while he
smoked and conversed perfunctorily with
Helen, was edging towards the 'schoolroom
end' of the veranda, presumably waiting for
the emergence of Miss Lawford and her
pupils — 'the truth is,' continued Mrs.
Cusack, 'that if I saw a decent excuse for
sending off Miss Lawford I should take it.
Unluckily, we are bound to each other for a
year's engagement; we thought, you know,

she might find the Bush dull—so many of
them do. But she has grown so flighty and
queer, and so up and down in her spirits,
that I don't consider her a good companion
for my girls. And I must say,' she added
severely, 'I think a certain gentleman is
much too fond of going home this way from
Ilganda, which is a great deal further round,
instead of taking the short-cut by the sur-
veyor's camp. I'm not one to suppose there's
any harm in an innocent flirtation, and Mrs.
Tregaskiss herself doesn't seem to mind it,
but still—anyhow, I don't intend to en-
courage it. I did hope that Miss Lawford
would take up with that old Land Commissioner, who is quite "gone" on her even
now; and he'd make her a very good husband. But it doesn't seem to come to anything, and the way she treats him is a shame.
I had to give her a talking to the other day
for making game of him as she does before
everybody.'

Mrs. Cusack rattled on for some time
upon the subject of Miss Lawford's delinquencies, then suddenly exclaimed:

'Keith Tregaskiss is sure to be making excuses for going over to Darra-Darra while she's there, and I'll tell you what you might do, Dr. Geneste. Mrs. Tregaskiss and Mrs. Hilditch were to have stayed with you before; I should feel much more comfortable if you had them now.'

'I don't know that Mrs. Tregaskiss would care to come,' said Geneste evasively; 'she is always busy at home.'

'A great deal too busy. I consider it scandalous, the way he keeps her without proper white servants, while he is going in for mining shares and pitching money about at Ilganda—I know it for a fact—and she, who, whatever sort of rogue her father might have been, was used to something very different! Don't you agree with me?'

'Mrs. Tregaskiss doesn't complain,' answered Geneste.

'No; I admire her for that. But now, look here, Dr. Geneste. Why shouldn't you get up that Lake Eungella picnic we've been talking about for ever so long? Though the weather is hot, one feels it less riding, and it's

nice and dry for camping. Helen's tremendously keen upon it ; and so is young Gillespie ;
and so was Mrs. Hilditch. I think the district ought to try and make Mrs. Hilditch's
visit a little more agreeable. Such a pretty
woman as she is ! And if she does lose her
money by marrying again, she might save
first out of her income, you know. I wish
there was a chance for Martin ; he's awfully
struck, I can tell you. Now, do him a good
turn, Dr. Geneste, and get them to come over.'

' Well, I will do my best.'

' That's right. I'm not sure that I shan't
try the picnic myself ; I don't think my riding
days are quite over yet. They tell me Lake
Eungella is a sight ; and you'll never do the
trip if you don't do it now before the rainy
season.'

' Do you think we shall have a rainy
season ?'

' Well, it doesn't look like it—worse luck !
But one goes on hoping, and when it does
come there'll be floods, and no mistake.
That's the way in Australia—waste or famine.
Mr. Cusack says that, if the drought doesn't

break up, it'll mean the ruin of every station with a heavy debt on it. I tell Mr. Blanchard that will be his time to invest.'

'Blanchard had better keep his eye on Darra-Darra if he is looking out for an investment.'

'Why, I know that Darra-Darra has got nothing of a debt. You don't mean that you are thinking of selling?'

'It is not very unlikely. I feel as though I ought to go back and have another try at the old country,' he replied vaguely.

That was how the report which reached Clare a few days later was started. Mrs. Cusack told the people at Brinda that she had it on Geneste's own authority he was going shortly to sell Darra and settle again in England; and Mr. Micklethwaite first carried it to Mount Wombo.

'Well, what do you think of the picnic?' continued Mrs. Cusack. 'Come over here, Nell, and persuade Dr. Geneste. We all want to be cheered up after the fire and the strike. I don't think Helen herself is looking as she should.'

'I am quite well,' declared Helen, growing red.

'Well, my dear, there's no disgrace in it. Now, just go and settle with Mr. Tregaskiss at once, doctor, and then write a note to his wife. You can't get out of it. Martin has set his heart on taking Mrs. Hilditch; he'll get the picnic up if you don't; and you are bound to have the whole lot of us for a night at Darra-Darra, anyhow. I'll send along a pack-horse with cakes and jam and goodies.'

'Would you like it?' asked Geneste of Helen.

'Very much indeed.'

'And shall I write to Mrs. Tregaskiss and ask her? I haven't seen her since poor Mrs. Carmody's funeral.'

'Oh yes, please; we could not go without her and Mrs. Hilditch,' said Helen.

Tottie and Minnie came out of the school-room, and were wild with delight at the prospect. Tregaskiss joined in. Of course, it was the very time for a spree; everybody had been in the dumps long enough. They'd make a big affair of it—the whole strength

of the three stations.   It wasn't such a bad
riding-track, and he knew of a splendid place
for a camp.   And they'd take their guns and
have some sport with pelicans.   And, then,
Geneste had never given a house-warming,
and here was an opportunity for entertaining
the district before the last batch of Specials
went away.   There should be a dance at
Darra-Darra.   Oh! he'd answer for his wife.
Of course, she and Mrs. Hilditch would be
there, and no doubt they'd stay the week if
Geneste liked.   Only he must bargain for
Ning ; he had promised the Pickaninny that
whenever that picnic came off she was to
ride to it.   By Jove! she was going to be a
magnificent horsewoman, that kiddie.   Her
mother didn't approve of her being out on
the run—said it would spoil her complexion
—make her back crooked—some rot of that
sort.   He intended that the girl should grow
up a sensible, strong woman, and none of
your weedy, sickly creatures.   Fortunately,
she had inherited his constitution.   He had
just broken in a filly for her—quiet as a
spaniel, and with paces that he'd wager

Cusack couldn't beat in all his famous breed, and so on. As for himself, he had been planning mustering that end of the run, and would begin next week. He'd be camped close to Darra, and would drop in and—he added jocularly to Minnie—see how they were getting on at lessons.

Mrs. Cusack interrupted him with severity.

' Now, look here, Mr. Tregaskiss, I think you had much better begin mustering at the other end of the run first. I dare say Mr. Cusack will lend you a hand or two if you want it. And, mind, I'm going over to take command at Darra-Darra, since Dr. Geneste hasn't got a lady of his own ; and I warn you that I shall decline to receive you unless you bring Mrs. Tregaskiss and Mrs. Hilditch. I don't approve of these gay bachelor outings of yours, and I don't believe in all your Ilganda business, either.'

Geneste did not write at once to Mrs. Tregaskiss. Keith went home that evening, and told his wife and Mrs. Hilditch that the Cusacks and Geneste were getting up a picnic to Lake Eungella ; and two days later one of the Cusack boys arrived with the same intelligence, supplemented by that additional piece of news about Geneste's contemplated abandonment of the Leura.

Mrs. Tregaskiss received the second edition of the report impassively, but she made an excuse before long to leave the veranda, where they were all sitting.

'What has become of Mr. Blanchard?' asked Mrs. Hilditch irrelevantly, as soon as she and Martin were alone. 'Why doesn't he come over here?'

'Oh, the Bishop! He's in the dumps—like the rest of us. We all hate being turned out of the quarters; we are cursing the Unionists all day and night—mostly night—when we are camped out looking for timber for the new wool-shed, and the mosquitoes have got their nippers into us. My word, Mrs. Hilditch, you should feel the mosquitoes' nippers out at Brigalow Creek!'

'I feel them quite enough here, thank you,' replied Gladys. 'I'm beginning to be very tired of the Leura, Mr. Martin, and you may tell Mr. Blanchard so. I shall go back to

England unless you do something at once to amuse me. You may tell Mr. Blanchard that, too.'

'Oh, but there's the picnic !' blurted Martin. 'And Geneste has half promised that we shall have a dance before the Specials leave altogether, and you will have to come to that, Mrs. Hilditch.'

'Dr. Geneste hasn't asked us yet ; I presume that he intends to. Nobody except Mr. Chance has been near us for ages; never in my life have I been so neglected. I'm obliged to feed my vanity on the compliments I get from the blacks' camp. You know, Mr. Martin, " Budgery White Mary, that fellow " becomes monotonous after you have heard it a good many times. Suppose you were to try, now, and give me a change ?'

Poor Martin got very red, and rubbed his forehead with his red silk pocket-handkerchief, becoming more confused still when he perceived that half the handkerchief had been torn off for stock-whip crackers.

'I wish you'd teach me how to make crackers,' said Gladys. 'And, look here,

Mr. Martin, I want you to take a message from me to Mr. Blanchard. Tell him that I particularly wish to see him before I go back to England. Tell him that I shall expect to meet him at Dr. Geneste's picnic. Tell him that I want to ask him what he would like me to say to his people about him. Do you understand?'

'Yes. I say, Mrs. Hilditch, is it true that Blanchard's relations are great swells, and that they have cut him because he got into a mess or something? I shouldn't have thought he was the sort of chap to get into a mess. His cobra is chock full of notions about what is right to do and what isn't. Perhaps you don't know that cobra is blacks' language for skull—do you?'

'Yes, I do. Ning taught me that, and I've been learning at the camp. Now go on.'

'Well, is it true?'

'Whether his relations are swells? Yes, I suppose you'd call them swells. His cousin is Lord Somebody, and, as he has got no children, the chances are Mr. Blanchard may be Lord Somebody, too, some day.'

' Oh, I say !'

' You won't chaff him now so much. I did think Australians were above that sort of snobbishness, but you're as bad as the worst of us over there.'

Martin looked abashed.

' You seem to get huffy if I ask you anything about Blanchard, so I won't talk about him.'

' No, don't. Yes, do. Tell me what it is like when you are camping out. Is he good company ?'

' First-rate,' rejoined Martin, ' when the mater is not by to chaff him. It's the mater and the old man who are the worst at it, and he always dries up when they're by. But you'd really be surprised at the lot Blanchard has got in his cobra.'

' Should I ?' said Gladys sarcastically.

' My word! yes. He let's you know he's about when it's a case of doing anything solid, or getting the rights off a chap. You should have heard him taking a rise out of Tummerill, the Government geologist.'

' That must have been very interesting. I should like to hear about that.'

'Old Tummerill was out prospecting, and he picked up a bit of burnt earth—stuff, you know, that cakes up in a hollow tree after the blacks have set fire to it. "That's volcanic lava," says Tummerill. "No," says the Bishop, "it's burnt stump." "What do you know about it?" says Tummerill; "I tell you it's volcanic lava." "Burnt stump," says the Bishop, and he stuck to it; and burnt stump it proved to be. Old Tummerill looked green, I can tell you. These geologist fellows seem to know precious little about their business,' sapiently concluded Martin.

Then Mrs. Hilditch artfully led the youth on to tell her more anecdotes about Blanchard, and on the whole enjoyed the hour she spent with him on the veranda more than she had enjoyed anything during the last three weeks.

And meanwhile Clare Tregaskiss was stretched upon her bed, the pillow stuffed into her mouth, her whole frame convulsed with tearless sobs. What was she to do? How was she to get rid of the pain? How was she to fight this awful thing which had taken possession of her? How was she to separate herself from him? How was she to conquer this love which was stronger than anything else in the universe except two little helpless babes? Oh! if it were possible —if only these two small creatures, who dragged at her, and held her from him, had no existence, then what bliss to do what he asked her — to yield up her life into his keeping.

CHAPTER XXVI.

AT DARRA-DARRA.

GENESTE's letter of invitation, when Jemmy
Rodd brought it, was friendly and formally
cordial, and conveyed little satisfaction to
Mrs. Tregaskiss. It had only two sentences
of balm :

' I hope that you will come. I have been
wishing very much that I might go and see
you.'

Clare was in the mood for heroism—a
mood born of passionate self-disgust ; and
her refusal would have been more than
probable but for certain compelling reasons
outside her own secret longing to see
Geneste. Tregaskiss insisted, Gladys insisted, and Ning insisted.

A little incident occurred about this time
which was also a strong determining influence.
Clare had always been given free access to
Tregaskiss' papers, station accounts, and so
forth, and had been in the habit of acting
more or less as his secretary. During any
press of cattle work she had taken entire
charge of his business correspondence.
Thus, one day when a summons to a meeting of the Pastoralist Committee interfered
with the drawing up of a certain statement
required by the Bank, it was quite natural
that he should desire her to overhaul the
ledgers and documents in his safe, and to
make out the statement ready for him on his
return. In her task Clare came upon the
letter he had begun to Hetty Lawford some
time before, and which he had thrust into the
safe on the report of the escape of the horses,
and had entirely forgotten.

Clare read the letter, not at first grasping
what its purport was, or to whom addressed.
The discovery of her husband's real feelings
affected her to a degree which she could
hardly have believed possible. She folded

up the letter, put it in an envelope directed to him, and laid it again in the safe, not in a position where it would be readily seen.

It was after the finding of this letter that a fit of recklessness came over her. Why should she struggle on along the difficult path of renunciation, torturing herself for the sake of a duty which her husband had renounced while she herself remained still loyal ? For the date of the letter showed her that it had been written upon the very night of that critical scene with Geneste, when for the first time they had exchanged assurances of love. Later, justice forced her to realize that in his nature, too, there had been a struggle simultaneous with that in her own ; but at first only the coarser aspects of the situation, as it involved him with Miss Lawford, presented themselves to her, and she felt a sense of outrage almost incommensurate with the wrong. In her spasm of indignant revulsion she wrote to Geneste accepting his invitation. So, with a guilty joy in her heart, and a great dread, she packed her saddle-bags—for it was arranged

that they were to ride to Darra-Darra, in
view of the camping-out expedition afterwards—and sent a message to Mrs. Ramm,
fortunately still camped between the two
stations, begging her to come over and take
care of the baby for four days.

Darra-Darra station ran into the hilly
country. The head-station was situated on
the very border of the plain on a sharply-
projecting knoll, two sides of which sloped
gently downward, while the other descended
abruptly to the level, presenting a precipice
very slightly softened by undergrowth, and
thus from a distance giving almost the
appearance of a fortification. The usual
lagoon lay at the foot of this knoll, and grape
vines, and recently planted fruit-trees, as
well as some older ones, ran down to it. On
a barren patch of ground, above the cliff,
grew several weird-looking, twisted, and
blackened grass-trees, which Geneste had
wisely allowed to remain. The house was
low, like all Australian houses, and zinc-
roofed, with deep verandas. It consisted of
two buildings—the new stone rooms, of which

Geneste had boasted, and the original cottage, dilapidated, and almost covered with creepers.

Besides these, there were the kitchen and the various outbuildings. Behind rose the lowest spurs of the range which had to be crossed before Eungella Lake could be reached, and in front stretched the brown, ocean-like plain.

The whole place, from its position, was peculiar and picturesque. A number of people on horseback met the Tregaskiss party when it was within a mile or two of the station. These were Helen Cusack, looking fresh and dainty in her holland riding habit and sun-bonnet; her two sisters, their un-bound manes flowing out as they cantered along; Miss Lawford, Martin Cusack, and Geneste. There were the conventional salutations and a mingling of parties, in a straggling line, till the paddock sliprails were passed through; then a dropping into twos, Martin Cusack and Gladys leading. It was natural that Mrs. Tregaskiss and her host should pair. Ning, on the quiet filly which

Tregaskiss had broken for her, dragged by her mother's side, more tired with her twenty miles than she would own, and put a slight restraint on the conversation.

Clare's gray veil was raised, and Geneste scanned her features.

'You are looking very unwell,' he exclaimed. 'Have you been fainting again? Yes, you need not equivocate. I know that you have.'

'It was not a bad attack. I did not mean to equivocate. The heat upset me, and baby has not been well; and things have been generally trying.'

'Do you know,' he asked abruptly, 'that it is just six weeks since Mrs. Carmody's funeral?'

'Yes.'

'Six weeks in which I have not heard your voice, nor looked on your face, nor had a line of your handwriting. It was cruel not to give me a word.'

'You never wrote to me.'

'I beg your pardon. I wrote you many letters, but I never sent one of them.'

'Ah! Why?'

'I was afraid that perhaps I had said in them what might offend you.' She was silent. 'Well,' he said, 'I have obeyed you.'

'Yes,' she answered.

'Surely, thou shalt praise me to-day, O Cæsar? Have you no commendation for me?'

'I can't. Surely you know——' She broke off. 'Have you seen—have you seen much of the Cusacks?'

'I have been over pretty often. Helen and Miss Lawford are staying here, while over there they are doing up the Bachelors' Quarters. And Martin comes backwards and forwards, and there are Tottie and Minnie to preserve the proprieties.'

Tregaskiss called out to Ning:

'Pickaninny, there's a log for you. Come and show Miss Lawford how I have taught you to jump.'

The child drew back; Clare and Geneste did not wait. They were now alone.

'Clare,' he cried, 'you have been very unhappy?'

'That is true,' she replied. 'Why do you torment me? Why will you not let us be friends?'

'I torment you! Yes, my dear'—his whole manner changed to that winning one which was so sweet to her—'let us be friends. I think in truth we must have been enemies during these long six weeks—these interminable weeks.'

'Tell me,' she asked, 'is it true—I heard through the Cusacks as a fact—that you are going soon to sell Darra and leave the Leura?'

'We talked of it, do you remember? Under certain conditions I think it is more than probable; but I have made no plans.'

'Under certain conditions!' she repeated, a terrified note in her voice.

He, wilfully misinterpreting it, exclaimed:

'Don't be afraid. I shall ask no more impossibilities; but,' he added in a lower tone, 'you must not expect impossibilities from me.'

They reached the entrance, and he became again the courteous host. After tea had been

taken in the veranda, and when dusk was
falling, it became a question of allotting rooms
to the guests, and Geneste turned to Helen,
not realizing the subtle and intense bitterness
there was to Clare in his manner of so doing.

'You and Mrs. Cusack settled things so
that Mrs. Tregaskiss would be as comfortable
as she could be in my bachelor diggings,' he
said.   'Mrs. Cusack has deserted us ;' and
he now looked at Clare.   'She said that we
should not want a chaperon now you were
here ; and she was afraid the men would put
up the wrong paper at Brinda.   We've had
to give up the notion of the ball,' he added,
as they walked along the veranda ; 'it was
too ambitious, and we were afraid it would
prevent the ladies from being fresh for
Eungella.   Besides, there were difficulties
about music, as I haven't got a piano.   However, Martin discovered a fiddle among the
Free Labourers at the Workings, and Blanchard is coming over later with the performer
in charge ; so perhaps, after all, we may
manage a very humble " hop " for the
children.'

He bowed at the door of a room in the stone buildings and left them.   Helen stood back for Mrs. Tregaskiss to enter.

' Oh, he has given me up his own room !' Clare said ; and her bitterness all went away; he had reserved this compliment for her, though, after all, it was the most natural thing in the world.   She knew that it must be his room, from the books and photographs and personal belongings.   Womanlike, she took note of all the little niceties.

' He would not hear of anything else,' answered Helen.   ' He wanted to give it up to mother, but she liked best being with me in my room.   Mother thought, Mrs. Tregaskiss, that you and Mrs. Hilditch and Ning could manage with this little dressing-cupboard, as the place is all rather crowded, and that Mr. Tregaskiss would be more comfortable in the Bachelors' Quarters, with the other gentlemen.'

Gladys was herself again, and yet not herself.   For the first time since her coming among them she put on a black dress, and it seemed to sober her and invest her somehow with a certain tragic dignity. It was a black dress, the like of which had never been seen upon the Leura—all soft dark filminess and indescribable folds, through which her white neck gleamed, and out of which emerged her bare round arms, with queer-looking bracelets clasping them above the elbow. Beside her Miss Lawford's costume of net and bugles and crimson satin ribbon looked tawdry and its wearer vulgar. Ambrose Blanchard watched Mrs. Hilditch as she came along the veranda, her delicate proud face and golden head rising out of the blackness of her gown, and thought of old Cyrus Chance's name for her, 'Fair Ines.' He thought of Felmarshes, and of her beauty and sweetness and passionate disdain of the sordid banalities of her life in those early days when she had been the ideal lady of his dreams. She had seemed to him then a being too refined, rare and exquisite for even the commonplace magnificence which surrounded her—a sort of queen who should just by right of nature possess everything that gold could buy, and yet despise all

material state and appanage. But deprived
of the state and appanage how could she
exist? She was poor now in comparison
with her former wealth. After all, five
thousand a year is not such a tremendous
income, though for a solitary woman it means
power to indulge in all manner of luxuries.
He shuddered as he felt himself assailed by a
fiercer temptation than any which had ever
visited him. Could he be so selfish and
cowardly as to take advantage of this beautiful
quixotic being, who, something told him,
would sacrifice readily for his sake all the
advantages of her position, and condemn her
to a lifetime of hardship, and probably of dis-
illusion?

Gladys went straight up to him and held
out her hand. She had schooled herself,
while she was dressing, for the meeting.

'You have not given me an opportunity of
thanking you for having dragged me out of
that dreadful burning room,' she said, quite
conventionally. 'I hope Mr. Martin gave
you my message.'

'Martin told me you were good enough

—that you wanted to see me,' he stammered.
' I am sorry not to have been able to come
over ; but——'

' Blanchard, will you give Mrs. Hilditch
your arm ?' said Geneste, passing on with
Mrs. Tregaskiss.

The dinner was a little constrained—the
party not large enough for collective hilarity
or for confidential duologue—and the conversation was mainly about the road to Lake
Eungella, the chance of rain in the hills
having swelled the lake, or of the drought
having dried it up, thus putting the mirage,
which was what everybody wanted to see,
out of the question. Of course, too, there
was a good deal of talk about the strike and
the rebuilding of the house and other local
topics, but it was all more or less forced.
Almost all present were preoccupied with
their individual anxieties—except, indeed, the
three or four Bushmen, Martin, Mr. Shand,
and some others, among them a late arrival
from the Gulf district, who had wonderful
tales about alligators and blacks, and other
horrors, to the edification of Ning and the

younger Cusack girls. Their end of the
table was very cheerful, but at the other,
Geneste and Mrs. Tregaskiss said little,
having always the shadow between them of
crisis, and perhaps impending separation.

Gladys and Mr. Blanchard were unnerved
by a sweet and terrifying agitation; and
Helen Cusack, thrilled with something of the
martyr's enthusiasm of renunciation, was yet
nervously eager to avert the declaration
which she knew young Gillespie was going
to make her; while Tregaskiss, in his rude
fashion, suffered from his own doubts, be-
wilderments, and emotions of various kinds.
In his breast surged unwonted feelings; he,
too, was undergoing the education of pain.
He felt anger, jealousy, miserable dissatisfac-
tion with himself and with all the world,
restless hunger for he scarcely knew what—
whether for his wife's affection or for a more
potent excitement. Anyhow, he had a reckless resolve to still at any cost the vague
remorse which was tormenting him. In an
odd, intuitive way, he divined something in
his wife's nature which had never shown

itself before these days—something which was not for him and had never been for him, and which was worth a million times more than the passive obedience, the half-reluctant acceptance of caresses that represented all the love she had ever given him. It angered him that the best of his own possessions should be, after all, but a shadowy possession —a thing to which he had the right in name and not in fact ; and, though he could not define his jealousy of Geneste, could not make out to himself any statement of injury, and did not suspect his wife of the least dereliction from the path of wifely honour, yet the consciousness of a wrong was always with him, and goaded him to seek sources of distraction, one of which, at any rate, was fairly effectual. In truth, of late, intemperance had become so much a habit with poor Keith Tregaskiss that, though he never openly disgraced himself, he was yet never wholly in his right mind.

'Will you come and look at my curios and Egyptian things?' Geneste said to Mrs. Tregaskiss when dinner was over and the party had dispersed—some to the garden to gather loquats and Cape mulberries, others to lounge and smoke and chatter about the veranda and steps, while the children and their traveller from the Gulf started a game of romps by moonlight. The dance had fallen through, after all, Martin's fiddler having been found to have 'gone on the spree.'

'I am not very sorry, said Geneste. 'I want you all to be as fit as you can be for the ride to-morrow.'

He had taken Mrs. Tregaskiss into what he called 'the office,' which was, however, very different from the usual station office—a receptacle for stock-whips and guns and a place in which to keep the ledgers. Geneste's office was lined with books, and had comfortable armchairs and some prettinesses; it was, in fact, where he spent most of his time indoors. She looked round it, examining the books and taking stock of everything, as a woman does of the place inhabited by the man she cares for.

He drew a chair forward and arranged the lamp.

'Sit here, and I'll put the things on this table for you. There's nothing really to look at—only a few odds and ends; and it was an excuse to bring you away.'

He unlocked some drawers and brought out coins and scarabei, and little souvenirs, mostly barbaric, from different countries he had visited. She examined the collection almost in silence; and he talked only conventionalities, telling her anecdotes about his properties and how he had acquired them. Suddenly she swept the whole subject away, as it were, with a wave of her hand, and got up, standing in front of the open door, which gave upon a quiet corner of the garden. The weird-looking grass-trees were silhouetted against the sky, and beyond stretched the great shadowy plain. To Clare that vast expanse of dead level meeting the sky seemed like the walled-in space of a gigantic prison.

'How can you endure to stay in this awful place,' she exclaimed, 'when you have the whole world before you to choose from, and when you know what's best in it to choose?—

not like Martin Cusack and Mr. Shand and
the others, who let their lives rust out from
sheer ignorance.'

He had risen and followed her.

' I have sometimes asked myself that question,' he said.

' Then go!' she said passionately, 'and let
us have done with this. In good truth it is
too hard for me to bear. I was better off in
the old lonely life than now, when I am
tossed, torn, tortured, and self-hating. I
think I'd rather be buried alive straight away,
and have the stone shut down upon me past
all hope, than live on in the agony I've been
enduring these last weeks. Oh! if I were in
your place I wouldn't bear it, either. No
woman is worth all that. See what I am
making you suffer now by my moods and my
complaints ; but I can't help it. I can only
say to you, " Go!"'

He came a little closer, and would have
answered her recklessly with an embrace ;
but she made an imperious gesture.

' No, no! I must not have that kind of
assurance. There'd be no arriving at any

conclusion if we let ourselves be swayed by feeling. Be patient with me, and self-restrained—as you have been. It is the truest proof of your affection.'

' Ah !' he exclaimed. 'And yet you yourself have taunted me with being no more than man.'

She gave him a melancholy smile.

' Be patient with me,' she repeated. ' Don't bring up my cruel speeches against me. I know what you feel now—at this moment that we are together. I know what you would say—that the happiness snatched at in rare meetings counterbalances the long pain. But it isn't so. You know, by all the light of your reason—as I know too well—that we cannot go on meeting without misery, danger, disaster—oh, yes, yes ! the worst disaster. I am weak. I can't trust myself—I can't trust you. I dare not let you come to my side and say all the tender things that are so sweet to hear. I dare not —that is the truth. And so you had better go, and leave me. I can bear more bravely to live my life alone.'

She had said all this in a low, agitated tone, not looking at him. Now she turned her eyes to his, and he was pierced by the despair in them.

'Oh, if I were only a man!' she cried vehemently. 'If I could only escape, as you might do! If I could just break away from everything, and roam—and roam—and never come back again!'

Her voice dropped in a long cadence, like the beat of a wild bird's wings; and she made a motion with her arms which reminded him of that moment of self-abandonment at The Grave, and touched him with something of her own despair.

'Clare!' he cried, 'you talk as if we couldn't help ourselves—as though we were bound by some grim fate to torture ourselves and each other, and it isn't so. The whole thing rests with you. If you choose, you can break away from everything, and we will roam—and roam—together.'

Again she silenced him by that quick gesture; and he remained waiting, not daring to say more till she should speak, or at least look at him. But she did neither—only leaned her head wearily against the edge of the door and looked out, her eyes seeming to pierce through far-reaching vistas, her chin slightly raised, and every feature ravaged by spiritual combat. He stood watching her, no less moved, but perfectly still. There was nothing in the attitude of either to rouse suspicion in an observer's mind of anything strained or unusual in their relation; but there was much in the expression of their faces.

CHAPTER XXVII.

BOTH Clare and Geneste had forgotten that their position in the lighted room made them an easy target for observation from the garden ; or, if the passing thought had occurred to Geneste when they came in, he dismissed it, remembering how little frequented was that side-bit of the garden.

As it happened, however, Tregaskiss had strolled hither with his pipe, and at that moment came within eye-range of the office door. He wanted to escape some disagreeable close-questioning of the Gulf traveller about a Northern gold-mine, in which he had been interested to a greater extent than he wished people to know, for it had turned out

a bubble. Moreover, he had other and more
unpleasant matters to ponder, for, just before
leaving Mount Wombo, he had received a
letter from the manager of his Bank, inform-
ing him of the impending visit of an inspector
to report on the security Mount Wombo now
offered for the original debt and increasing
over-draft. He had been nursing his irrita-
tion till it had become a smouldering fury,
and the scene which he surprised was like a
match set to inflammable material. He had
been looking for Clare in order that he
might tell her this piece of bad news, and
thus vent some of his annoyance ; and he
had been much displeased at the arrangement
which located him among the bachelors far
from her. Now he found her as she stood
sideways against the door, her unseeing eyes
fixed outward beyond him, not listless and
indifferent, as he had expected, but alive and
quivering with some strange and, for the
moment, to him incomprehensible emotion.
He had never seen the shadow of such a
look upon her face before—the light fell upon
her, and he could read every lineament. It

seemed to lift her to a region far, far away
from the hardships and worries of their
common lot. She would not care, he told
himself bitterly, if he were ruined to-morrow,
or killed, for that matter. She was absorbed
by some overmastering feeling, of which he
had no knowledge, which had nothing to do
with him or her married life. He realized
that at this moment he himself was no more
to her than the dust she might shake off her
feet. What did it mean? What had happened to her?

Then he caught sight of Geneste, too, and
the whole thing flashed upon him. In a
second he was given the key to much that
during all their life together had irked and
puzzled him in Clare, and that of late had, in
a manner for which he could hardly account,
stirred up the brute and the devil in himself.
Her stillness, her coldness, her apathy, her
queer notions, as he called them, conveyed to
him more by her reserve on some topics than
by actual words, and which had made him
call her 'uncanny.' Everything in her that
had baffled him, and had caused him to feel,

in a dull way, that his marriage was an in-
complete thing, seemed to become clear,
revealed in those two faces.

Clare had never cared for him ; she had
always despised him, and she had only kept
silence, and pretended to be loyal, as long as
she despised everybody else on the Leura,
since she considered none worthy of being
her confidant. But Geneste was different.
From the first, Tregaskiss told himself, he
had seen that she was trying to prove to
Geneste how superior she was to her husband
and to her surroundings—exalting herself at
his, Tregaskiss', expense. He had formerly
derived a certain satisfaction, mingled with
his discontent, at her aloofness. If she were
cold and, as he fancied, contemptuous sometimes to him, she was disdainful to everybody
else ; and, at any rate, this peculiarity in her
implied on his part the possession of a super-
fine article, of which he was undisputed
master, and might claim all the glory. But
now he realized that he was not Clare's undisputed master ; that someone else had the
power to lift her out of her stately, impassive

self; that her whole being was in rebellion against him; and that she did indeed hold him in contempt—there was the sting to Tregaskiss; despised his manners, his want of intellectuality—even his physical strength and comeliness. And on occasions, when he had bragged about her to Geneste, as was a way of his—Candaules fashion—Geneste had, no doubt, laughed at him in his sleeve—Tregaskiss writhed at the thought—knowing well how Clare felt. Tregaskiss' jealousy was not of the ordinary conjugal kind. In a curious way he had been pleased that Geneste should admire Clare—should even fall in love with her; that was a tribute to himself. It was of his power over her that he was jealous, and he was more bitter against Clare than against Geneste.

Some two-edged remarks that Geneste had incautiously made to him, certain sayings of the Cusacks, and of Miss Lawford, which he had not made much of at the time, but which had festered, nevertheless, came back and strengthened his case against his wife. She was making him the laughing-stock of

the district. This was the meaning of all
that dangling at Mount Wombo—'sentiment-
ality and rot,' as he put it—at the time of her
attack of fever, which he had not believed in.
Geneste was in love with his wife. Most
probably he had told her so. Now Tregaskiss said to himself that he understood the
cessation of intimacy during these last weeks.
There was no doubt that Clare had a sentimental fancy for the man : her face told him
that; but, no doubt, too, she had gone into
heroics, and mounted her virtuous horse, and
sent him away. That would be like Clare.
She would do her duty, and, he added in a
sort of *sotto voce*, be 'damned unpleasant'
about it. She was not the woman to go off
the rails ; she had not the temperament.

Tregaskiss argued upon his own experience
of the limitations of her temperament, as
husbands, who consider their wives beyond
temptation, are wont to do. It was very
curious how, in all his anger and jealousy,
he never suspected his wife or Geneste of
any serious lapse from rectitude. Indeed,
their impeccability, as he believed it, roused

more of the wicked feelings in him. In a
perverse way, he could have found in their
strayings justification for his own deviation
from the straight path. In that mood of
his, he would have been glad—and yet the
thought was hell!—of a legitimate outlet
for all the morbid passions that swelled in
him.

But there was nothing, no reasonable
excuse for rushing in and assaulting Geneste,
if he had been so minded. Besides, he was
a coward, and cowards always prefer to bully
a woman. The two he was watching stood
apart; they had not even touched hands.
There was nothing to betray them but their
faces : hers with that wonderful emotion
transfiguring it—passion, longing, disgust,
unutterable weariness of the very air she
breathed, and of the great plain which was
her prison—that was how he interpreted it,
with a more correct divination than might
have been expected of him ; and Geneste's,
no less agitated, telling of a conflict which
Tregaskiss read, according to his material
interpretation of things, as the struggle of

rebuffed desire.   Of course Clare had rebuffed him.   Tregaskiss could imagine the
pleading and the answer; but the pleading
had stirred in her a consonant chord of
passion.

'Infernal puppy!' muttered Tregaskiss.
And yet his distorted notion of revenge
fixed itself upon Clare, and not upon the
man, with whom, in truth, he had something of the man's sympathy—upon Clare,
in whose innocence he, nevertheless, firmly
believed.   What right had she to be setting
herself above everybody else ?—giving herself confounded airs of superiority, and sneer-
ing at other women who were human ?   He
remembered a look across the dinner-table—
a glance only—which he had intercepted on
its way to Miss Lawford.   He made a step
forward, with the half-intention of confront-
ing the two, calling her out to him, and
proving his ownership.   Then a change of
attitude in the man he was watching arrested
him.   Geneste said something to Clare in a
low voice—Tregaskiss could not hear the
words—and she turned and answered him

hurriedly — it seemed entreatingly. And
then Geneste quietly left her, closing the
door behind him.

It was not much of a scene to build a
tragedy on. What had really happened just
then was, as Tregaskiss conjectured, that
Geneste had become aware, somehow, of his
presence in the garden, and had begged
Clare to return with him to the veranda, and
she had bidden him leave her till she could
face the others more composedly. She moved
from the window and stood by the table on
which the curios were still spread out. She
could hear her husband's step now scrunch-
ing the gravel, though she was not certain
that it was he. At any rate, she was not
going to fly away like a frightened schoolgirl, and so waited for him till he had
reached the log-steps that led straight into
the garden. Tregaskiss stood there a moment, and took his pipe out of his mouth,
shaking a shower of red ashes to the ground.

' I want to speak to you,' he said.

She knew by his voice that he was not
in command of himself, and merely bowed

her head.   He stepped into the room beside
her.

'Look here,' he said : 'I'll not have you
whining and complaining about me, making
yourself out an injured martyr and me a
brute.   Do you suppose I can't guess what
you've been talking about to Geneste ?
Getting him to pity you—we all know what
that leads to.   He's in love with you ; you
can't deny it.   Very well ; if it amuses you,
carry on as much as you please, and take
the consequences.   But don't presume to
find fault with me, and don't think that I'm
going to be made a fool of, and ridden
rough-shod over.   If you do, you are very
much mistaken.   Do you hear ?'

She drew herself together with a little
shiver, but did not answer.   Her silence
goaded on Tregaskiss.

'Do you hear ?' he repeated.   'I have
found you out at last.   I know how you
have been working against me—spoiling my
credit in the district.   Old Cyrus Chance
first—curse him !   Do you fancy he's going
to leave you any money for it ?—and the

Cusacks and Geneste. Just, too, when I want to raise some money to get me out of a hole and keep the Bank from coming down on me! And then setting my own child against me! Telling Ning she's not to do what I want; forbidding her to go out walking with Miss Lawford; making out that her father's friends aren't good enough for her; signalling to her to come and stop by you when she is quite happy with me and the people I like. You thought I didn't see you! Oh, I can read you through and through! I know your underhand ways— too mean to say a thing out. But to set the pickaninny against me—that's what I won't stand! No; I'm damned if I do!'

'I have never done any such thing, Keith, as to set your child against you; and what you say is like a madman's talk.'

'You'll tell me I'm drunk, I suppose. That's what you are always insinuating. And you've been telling Geneste the same thing—taking away my character behind my back. Will you swear to me that you've never said a word against me to him? Come,

you daren't ; you know that I could bring
witnesses forward to prove that you've be-
littled me to the Cusacks. What were you
talking about before I came along and saw
you both standing here ? Will you swear
that you never told him I drank too much
and was unkind to you ? Come, answer me.'

She made no reply.

'Answer me !' he cried again. 'When I
was away that time, and you pretended to
be ill, you made out your case—didn't you,
now ? I'm a brute and you are immaculate.
And I took you away from your English
comforts and grandeur—forced you to marry
me, eh ! and buried you in this hole of a
district, and treat you no better than a black
gin—don't give you decent white servants—
that's your cry to Mrs. Cusack ; oh ! I've
heard all about it—when you know that I
have offered you a proper white nurse scores
of times ! You didn't say a word, did you,
about your thief of a father ? Didn't tell
them that I took pity on you when your
other lover cast you off, and all your fine
friends would have nothing to say to you ?

Where would you be now if I hadn't come forward like the fool I was? You didn't despise me then, nor the Leura neither. This is your gratitude; and you haven't got a word to say for yourself. You're ashamed to look me in the face.'

Still she was silent; but she made a movement as if she would have left the room. He caught her arm.

'I will have an answer. By —— ! I'll not have dirt thrown at me behind my back without punishing you, and knowing the reason why.'

'You are hurting me! You insult me! Keith, don't! You make me hate you!'

'I thought as much. You've hated me all these years; when I've been sweating to get things for you, loading you with kindness. And you've been working against me in the dark; poisoning the pickaninny's mind against her father — the pickaninny, who's the thing I care for most in the world. If it wasn't for the pickaninny I'd cut the whole concern to-morrow, and be happy in my own way, and let you go yours, and be damned to you. I'm sick of it all, I tell you—sick of you, sick of your cold, stand-off, contemptuous ways. I'm glad you've spoken out at last. You hate me, do you? Very well. I hate you, and that's the honest truth ; and you may go to —— for all I care. Get out of my sight, you mean, skulking devil!'

He loosed his hold on her arm as he poured forth the evil words. And then, to the disgrace of his manhood, poor, mad, half-drunken Tregaskiss lifted his hand and struck his wife. He had lost all control over himself; the proportions of things were all clouded and distorted to his inflamed, drink-saturated brain. Never before had he spoken to her in this way, violent as he had sometimes been, and never before had he raised his hand against her. The shock of it seemed for the moment almost more than she could bear. She staggered, and turned very white. The blow tingled on her shoulder beneath her thin dress, and made a great red patch under the gauze. He looked at her for a second abashed at what he had done, but

something seemed to come between her and
and him blur and blotch her image, distort-
ing it like his own fancies of her, and the
brute in him kept the upper hand.

'Go and tell him that, too, and then let
him come and settle things with me. I'm
ready for him!'

'Yes,' she said, almost in a whisper, from
the intensity of her scorn and hate, 'I will
tell him; and from to-night, Keith, all is
ended between you and me.'

She went past him, and down the steps
into the garden, then along the gravel path
by the back of the house to the end of the
big veranda from which her own room
opened. She could see the flutter of dresses
away down the garden, and could hear the
laughter of the two little Cusack girls, and
the sound of Ambrose Blanchard's voice,
singing a love-song, in the drawing-room at
the other end of the veranda. The night was
young yet; these people were amused and
occupied; it would be a long time before they
thought of bed.

She crept into her room. Oh, the relief

of knowing that this night, at least, her
husband would not share it with her! Ning
lay fast asleep in the stretcher-bed that had
been improvised for her in the bath-room
adjoining, her little limbs half uncovered, and
her elfish locks streaming about the pillow.
Gladys' bed had the mosquito-nets drawn
close, and was, of course, empty. Clare
determined that she would get into her own
bed and pretend to be asleep, so that Gladys
might not ask her any questions. She took
off her dress, and stood before the glass looking at herself— at her stony face, in which the
eyes were like living things, so bright were
they, and at the cruel red mark upon the
whiteness of her neck. The thought came
to her that it might be well Gladys should
see that mark. She remembered Geneste's
suggestion about the possibility of legiti-
mately gaining her freedom ; but she dismissed the notion as though it had been a
guilty one. That would be mean indeed—
at least, so it seemed to her.

For, through all her outraged dignity and
woman's revolt against his treatment, her

conscience found excuses for Tregaskiss. He had upbraided her coarsely, and, in one sense, wrongfully, and he had struck her; but, in another sense, had she not deserved the upbraidings, and, according to rough-and-ready ethics, the blow? She had not taken her husband's character away to Mrs. Cusack, nor had she ever tried to set his child against him; but had she not been false to her wifely vow in a far worse way? Had she not allowed herself to consider as a possibility— nay, was she not even now almost, in her heart, consenting to that which would give him a right to punish her by separating her for ever from her children? He had not accused her of the greater wrong; he had faith in her so far—which was, in its way, noble of him, magnanimous—and through everything it touched her. It was for the paltry, ignoble cause that he had struck her. There was bathos in the combination of ideas which, in spite of the tragedy of the situation, made her laugh aloud in grim amusement.

She blew out the light when she was in

bed and lay quite still, the moonlight streaming in through the creepers which screened
the veranda, and making a vine-leaf pattern
on the floor. The bruise on her shoulder
smarted, and forced her thoughts back, in
spite of herself, to that scene with her
husband, which, as she went over and over
it with all the unconscious exaggeration of
recent happening, seemed to her, putting
aside all else that was involved, to have
altered the whole course of her life. Never,
she told herself, could they two live together
again in amity, or even peace. She was a
woman of great self-control, slow to wrath,
and not given to denunciation or meaningless
declaration. She had said words to him
which to her were of momentous issue and
which could never be unsaid. She had told
him that he made her hate him; and he in
return had said that he hated her. How
could they pretend any longer? Whatever
happened, those words would always come
up between them and make union seem the
more horrible, because each would know that
they were true. For it was the truth—it had

always been the truth. Their characters and temperaments were antagonistic to the core, and Nature would have her way. Truth would out at last, however rigorously and however long it might be kept sealed within its prison.

'Yes, I do hate him!' the poor quivering thing whispered to herself as she lay huddled up, the sheet drawn over her face to hide it from the moonlight, and a fierce feeling of relief came to her in this giving vent to her secret thought, as when she had whispered to herself of another man : 'Oh, I do love him —I do love him!'

By-and-by Gladys came in. She was humming a little song—the one Blanchard had been singing—in the way that girls do when their hearts are light from the meeting with their love. Gladys felt like a girl this evening, and her heart was relieved of a great oppression. She, too, stood and looked at herself, and smiled happily at her own image. There were no tragic thoughts in her mind ; she had passed that phase of life ; it had come to her early, and was all over

now.   Clare thought bitterly that Fate had
let off Gladys easily, but Clare did not know
that the burden of a man's death lay upon
Gladys' soul.

Gladys did not at first remember her
friend, so taken up was she with her own
pleasant imaginings.   But presently, with a
little start of recollection, she turned, and
called softly ' Clare !' stooping when she got
no answer, and peering through the curtains
to satisfy herself that Mrs. Tregaskiss was
asleep.   She stopped singing, and moved
about very quietly in her preparations for
rest.   When the candle had been blown out
again there was a silence, and Clare, opening
her eyes, beheld Gladys — sophisticated,
cynical Gladys—kneeling in her nightdress
at the side of her bed, and saying her
prayers as humbly as any innocent child.
The sight wrung Clare's heart anew, and
brought home to her with startling reality
the ghastly incongruity of her own position.
Gladys was praying—no doubt for Ambrose
Blanchard and for herself—praying that a
blessing might attend their love ; praying

out of the fulness of her heart, and in the
conviction that there was nothing in it unworthy to be brought before the High
Throne. Oh, how crooked, how wrong, it
all seemed! That Gladys might thus pray—
Gladys whom death had freed; and that she,
Clare, who loved no less, but more absorb-
ingly; and no less purely—for love which
has its root in the affinity of souls must, she
told herself, be pure—she who was separated
from her husband by as hideous a gulf as
even death could make, might not put up a
petition, unless it were for strength to re-
nounce what seemed to her then dearer
than heaven—strength that she might keep
true to what had become an unnatural
duty.

CHAPTER XXVIII.

'TURN AGAIN, FAIR INES!'

HUSBAND and wife exchanged no word in private on the following morning. They were all to start for Lake Eungella at ten o'clock, and everyone was busy preparing for the camping out. The yard was full of horses; saddles were being seen to; pack-horses loaded; valises strapped up, and rations given out.

Tregaskiss came in late for breakfast, and was met by jocular upbraidings from the Gulf traveller for having spoiled his night's rest.

'You never saw such a chap, Mrs. Tregaskiss, for I'm sure he doesn't play on those larks when you are by to keep him in order,' said the Gulf man, with ill-timed pleasantry. 'Backed himself against each of us for a round with the gloves by moonlight, which was too much of a good thing at getting on for morning. We compromised on breakdowns—didn't you hear us up at the house? Then I'm blest if he didn't start on 'The Sick Stock-rider' when we were all ready to turn in, and led the chorus in a way that moved us to tears! I could never have given him credit for so much sentiment; but it was after the grog had been finished up, wasn't it, Tregaskiss? Looks a bit seedy this morning, don't he? I say, Martin, we shall be having the Bishop down on us for that breakdown!'

'The Bishop wasn't there,' said Martin. 'He cleared off to his own camp before we began to get rowdy. He wouldn't have a bunk in the quarters, Geneste, but said that as he was going to camp out to-night, and had been camping out for the last three weeks with the timber-cutters, he'd as well not make a change.'

Though Tregaskiss certainly looked haggard and out of sorts, he still seemed in

wild spirits.   He laughed and bragged, and
rollicked with Ning—making a show which
was almost ostentatious of his devotion to the
child—and except that he avoided looking
at or addressing his wife, no one would have
suspected that there was any family discord.
Helen had got into a way of peering below
the surface of things, and guessed that there
had been a serious disagreement ; while Mrs.
Hilditch had already learnt that when Tregaskiss was in a peculiarly irritable and rasp-
ing humour in private, it was his custom to
exhibit in public a boisterous geniality.   In
that irritable mood Tregaskiss seemed to find
a certain excitement in making a quarrel
with his wife ; he was like a dog worrying a
bone in the way that he harped upon a
grievance.   His grievances were always of a
petty nature, not worth serious dissension—
the cooking of a dish, the delinquencies of a
black-boy or stockman, some small domestic
neglect, or a difference of opinion on the
subject of Ning's bringing-up.   Gladys concluded that his bone in the present instance
had been Clare's objection to the long ride

for the child. There had been some talk about it at dinner the previous evening, and Geneste had then proposed that he should drive Ning the first ten miles in his buggy, till the road became impassable for wheels, so that the day's journey might be made easier.

The child, dressed in her little riding-habit, sat by her father's side, and was injudiciously fed by him with all the dainties the table showed forth. Mrs. Tregaskiss went to her room to finish her packing; and though Geneste had seen by her face that something was terribly wrong, he had no opportunity of saying a word to her before they started. Clare was riding his horse—the one he had lent her for the ride to the Carmodys' on that melancholy return from Brinda Plains. She attached herself to the Gulf man, as being the least likely of the party to notice her altered manner; but when the buggy came to a stop at a crossing which was only possible on horseback, and Ning was mounted on her filly, the party reconstructed itself. The tract now became tor-

tuous and steep, and the riders were obliged
to go in single file or else in twos, which often
lost sight of the rest of the company among
the trees.   It was wild country through which
they were passing.   A little beyond Darra-
Darra Station the plains had been left behind, and the grassy valleys and wooded
slopes through which they had come during
the first few miles ended when the buggy
turned back again.   Now they were among
barren ranges, sparsely timbered ; sometimes
along a bit of level road, or a tiny flat where
huge ant-beds of brown clay were scattered
about like gigantic heaps of caked mortar left
by an army of departed workmen.   Boulders
of rock lying here and there like rough-hewn
pillars helped the illusion.   Sometimes they
went by a shelving siding, with red cliffs
rising above their heads ; sometimes down a
rocky gorge or the course of a gully, where
the long-bladed grass grew rank and brown ;
and sometimes they would mount a precipi-
tous incline, which obliged them to lean
forward and grasp the horses' manes to keep
their seats.   Fortunately all were good riders,

even Mrs. Hilditch's horsemanship being beyond criticism.

She was riding a good way ahead—just behind the black-boys—with Ambrose Blanchard. Both were in light vein. Gladys' laugh rang out above the whirring of the locusts, and Ambrose every now and then would troll back a jodelling note or a line from an Australian song. These two seemed to have made a temporary truce with doubt and regret, and to have resolved upon taking the good of to-day without reference to the possible ill of to-morrow. Geneste and Mrs. Tregaskiss followed them. Behind came Helen and Harold Gillespie; and Helen was trying to keep Mr. Shand and the Gulf traveller within earshot, to stave off the sentimental interview which she knew Gillespie had in his mind. The others were 'dodging about,' as Martin put it—the little Cusack girls jumping convenient logs and riding tilt at hanging blossoms; the young men making short excursions after kangaroos, and otherwise bringing on themselves the reproach of taking too much out of their horses. Tre-

gaskiss joined sometimes in these romps, but
more often loitered with Miss Lawford in the
rear of the rest. He was smoking continu-
ously all the time, and got off occasionally,
and, on the pretext of tightening his girths,
took a pull at his flask.

As the noonday heat quenched frolicsome-
ness, voices grew subdued, and only the
beat of the horses' hoofs sounded among the
murmurs and rustling and whirrings of the
Bush. Gladys and Ambrose talked in a soft
undertone of all the pleasant things under
heaven. He had said to her as yet no
further word of love, but she knew that she
was forgiven for the past, and that her com-
panionship was a joy to him. No allusion
was made to Felmarshes, or to poor dead
Ironside; a tacit agreement seemed to have
been made between them the previous evening that the past was to be buried. Yet now
Gladys turned suddenly to him, and said
impulsively :

'Mr. Blanchard, will you tell me whether
you are glad or sorry that I came out to
Australia ?'

'Do you need to be told?' he answered.
'Don't you know that I shall never cease to
bless that night of the fire at Brinda Plains?
I am sorry that there was a fire, for the sake
of the Company, which will give a lesser divi-
dend this year; but I am wicked enough to
be glad for my own.'

He paused, and got suddenly red. He had
been thinking only of those blessed moments
when he had held Gladys in his arms, and
poured forth into her unconscious ears the
love which filled his heart. Were they quite
unconscious? He had fancied a faint pressure of her inert hand, that lay loosely upon
his shoulder. And then he remembered that
he had had no right thus to take advantage
of her helplessness, and added awkwardly:

'I mean that I can never be thankful
enough to you for showing me a part of
yourself which I had never understood
before.'

'That would have happened just the same
if there had been no fire,' said Gladys, with
some archness, 'and the poor shareholders
would not have lost their dividends.'

They were both silent for a minute or two, and then Gladys began again, a little tremulously :

'You must always think badly of me, as I used to be in the old days ; but tell me that you won't think quite as badly as you did before. Tell me that, at any rate, you believe in my sincerity towards you.'

'I believe in it entirely ; and I thank Heaven for it !'

'We are friends, then '—and she half reined in her horse and stretched out her hand to him across the pommel of her saddle—' friends as we used to say we meant always to be in those far-back days at Felmarshes !'

He took her hand in his, pressed and released it, and, though he said not a word, there was a look in his eyes which made Gladys' heart glad.

'Promise me, then,' she went on, 'that from to-day you will begin afresh with me, and that you will forget all the cruel thoughts you have been keeping of me in these years. Tell me that you will think of me now as one who, having made a bad mess of her life at

the start, wants to try and make as good a
thing as she can of it for the end.'

'Don't!' he exclaimed impetuously. 'It's
hard on me when you know that I must
always stand out of your life, and that it
would be happiest for me if I could bring
myself never to think of you at all—or only
as a beautiful dream. The end!'—and he
gave a little dreary laugh—'why do you talk
of the end, when you are at the beginning,
and have the whole world before you, and
everything it can give you in your power?'

'Have I?' she answered wistfully, and
laughing drearily, too.

'You have youth, money, intellect, charm,
sympathy, opportunity, and — freedom.
Doesn't that mean that everything is in your
power?'

'Everything in my power!' she repeated.
'Except the two things which, at present, I
most want to be able to do.'

'What are they?'

'I will tell you one. I should like to be
able to make Clare Tregaskiss happy.'

'Ha! I am afraid, indeed, that would be

out of the power of anyone but a magician,
unless all the conditions of her life could be
altered.'

' I would be a magician, and all the conditions of her life should be altered.   I would
sweep away everything — everybody — her
husband—Ning—the baby—the Leura. I
don't mean that I would do anybody bodily
harm. I would simply arrange things so
that nothing of all that existed—so that Mr.
Tregaskiss had never met Clare, and so that
he were married to somebody else who suited
him better—say Miss Lawford. If one were
a magician, it would be so easy; and a little
juggling and annihilation, more or less,
wouldn't matter.'

' If you swept away the Leura, as you say,
you would be annihilating a good many more
people than Keith Tregaskiss and his children. For one thing,' he added shyly, ' you
would be sweeping away—me.'

' No ; I should have worked my other will
by that time—you would not be here.'

' Will you tell me, Mrs. Hilditch, what you
would do with me if you were a magician ?'

Gladys hesitated, and blushed a little.

'If I were a magician,' she said softly, 'I would put you at home again, in your rightful place : not as a clergyman—oh no !—but reconciled to your father, and making a better sort of career for yourself than helping to cut down timber to rebuild the Brinda Plains Company's wool-shed, and carrying rations to shearers.'

'Perhaps,' he answered gently, 'that would be doing me a more cruel kindness than if you were to leave me here on the Leura to my timber-cutting and ration-carrying. Setting everything else aside, in England I should always be tormented by the tantalizing vision of a happiness which honour, conscience, all right, manly feeling must make it impossible for me even to think of.'

'Why impossible ? If—if one chooses, everything is possible.'

'You told me yourself a moment ago that your own dearest wish was an impossible one. Gladys,' he cried, 'you must know what I mean. You must know that to see you free, courted, and to love you as I love you, with absolutely no hope of winning you, would make life near you a hell to me.   I had better far rot my days out completely beyond reach of you, on a Western sheep-station.   There could be no opportunity then for jealous longings.'

' But if,' Gladys said falteringly—' if I preferred staying on the Leura to going back to England—if, having tried what civilization and money and all the rest could do for me, I had found it dust and ashes, and so determined to give the whole thing up and settle in a purer, freer atmosphere——'

' Oh yes,' he interrupted.   ' Among the mosquitoes and snakes and scorpions and blacks—with droughts and strikes and fires for agreeable interludes in the summer heat.'

' You may laugh if you please ; but I meant what I said,' she exclaimed hotly.   ' I don't mind droughts and heat and mosquitoes ; and as for strikes and fires, they are very agreeable excitements.   Yes, if I were to buy a station of my own, I dare say my trustees would advance me the capital——'

' On your solemn undertaking never

to marry again,' he interrupted a second
time.

'It does not seem that I shall need to give
that,' retorted Gladys bravely. 'The men
who care for me are either too mercenary or
too cowardly to take me without my money—
which I hate,' she added passionately. 'Yes,
I hate it ; I hate my money—it has come to
me in an unworthy way ; it is the price of
everything that should have been dearest
to me, and prevents me from throwing off
all the dreadful past and beginning a new,
good, happy life with no falsehood or pretence—the sort of life to make you glad,
Ambrose, that you had known me. Ah !
you don't believe that I am capable of living
that life ?'

'I believe you capable of everything that
is noble,' he said huskily.

'And yet you won't help me ; you let my
wretched money stand between us.'

'Yes,' he said, shutting his lips tight for
a moment in desperate determination. 'Your
money stands between us, and always must.'

'And,' she went on, 'what shall you say

if I do buy that Leura station and plant myself near you?   Unless you run away to England, then, you can't put yourself out of my reach.'

'It is not possible that you can be so cruel.'

Gladys laughed.   What did she care about anything in the world now that he had told her he loved her?   The rest would come right, must come right, since she was a woman who knew her power, and he was no more than human.

At her laugh Blanchard spurred his horse, and, purposely to avoid betraying himself further, made a dash through a belt of gidia to where a native creeper hung its wreath of blossoms over the shattered limbs of a tree which had been destroyed by a stroke of lightning.   He gathered a bunch of the flowers and brought them back to Gladys.

'They are very sweet,' he said in his ordinary tone, 'and not common about here. We haven't so many sweet-smelling things on the Leura when the sandal-wood is out of bloom.   You will see that the vegetation of the hills is a little different from that on the plains. What are they shouting about, I wonder?' he added, as the black-boys with the pack-horses, who had drawn up a little way ahead, sent out one of their peculiar blacks' cries. 'I suppose that we are in sight of the lake.'

Tregaskiss pressed past them trotting, leading Ning by the bridle-rein. The child was tearful with fatigue.

'There's a plucky one, Pickaninny!' he shouted. 'Come along! we're close up to camp. Now, Mrs. Hilditch, lay on like blazes to your horse's mane and take a lesson from Ning; we've got to get up that place.'

'That!'

Gladys looked in wonder at a steep ridge, with a razor-back top, rising quite abruptly from the more gentle slope they had been mounting. The side was almost a precipice, and gave the effect of a natural wall blocking their way. The growth of stunted gidia parted below the cone, and she saw that the range fell away on either side as though it had been cut, and that to right and left were

deep, impassable gorges.   It seemed to her
that from one of them the roar of a waterfall
sounded.

'Are we at the end of the world?' she
asked.

'We are close up to the top of the range,
and over it is the camp I said I was going to
bring you to,' replied Tregaskiss.   'Look
out there, Shand, confound you! Just you
take a back seat with the new-chums for a
bit!   I'm boss of this show, and I don't allow
any of you to come in front of the pickaninny!
I promised her she should have first show of
the lake, and Miss Lawford is to come next;
and, damn it! I'm going to keep to my word.
Come along, Hetty.'

The governess, who had been following
close behind Ning, gave a half-ashamed, half-
apologetic laugh.

'You mustn't mind Mr. Tregaskiss, Mrs.
Hilditch,' she said awkwardly.   'He is so
excited at having found us such a nice camp
that he has forgotten his manners.   Please go
first.'

Gladys reined in her horse and looked at

Miss Lawford with a calm air of aloofness, saying, with formal courtesy :

'No, pray follow Mr. Tregaskiss.'

Miss Lawford blushed deeply, and gave another hysterical giggle.

'Oh, it was only on Ning's account that I have kept forward ; the child has set her heart on getting the first sight of the lake.'

Gladys made a frigid bow, and pointedly drew back. Miss Lawford switched her horse, and, taking a zigzag line, mounted fearlessly after Tregaskiss. She was a magnificent Bushrider, and her little lithe body swayed with every movement of the animal. Tregaskiss, turning round, called out :

'Well done, Hetty !'

His rough ejaculations, as he dragged at Ning's bridle and encouraged the filly to flounder forward, reached Clare below, as in some anxiety she watched the child's ascent. The climb was a stiff one, and would have frightened a timid rider. Helen Cusack, who, though she was a Bush girl, had never gone after stock or sat a 'pig-jump,' far less a real 'buck-jump,' shrank a little. It was

Geneste who turned back, and, seizing her
bridle, helped her to the summit.   Mrs. Tregaskiss, with set lips and hard eyes, dashed
on ; she was in the mood to ride up a precipice, without caring whether the chances were
in favour of her reaching the top or being
hurled to the bottom.

The first cry of delighted surprise at the
view below came from Ning.

'Oh, the sea ! the sea !' she called out,
unconsciously echoing the shout of the Ten
Thousand.

There lay the lake, a great silvery sheet,
the opposite shore only dimly visible—a shore
of low hazy mountains, like clouds upon the
horizon.   A faint breeze tossed the waters
into miniature wavelets ; and brooding upon
them were immense flocks of wild-duck, black
swans, and different kinds of gulls, while on
the sandy beach strange, ungainly-looking
pelicans swelled their huge gullets and preened
their long curved beaks.

The cone on which they stood was at the
bend of a curve, and beyond the gorges on
each side of it the range sloped down from its

razor-back summit in long undulations, cut
here and there by deep furrows, with green
pastures in the openings at the foot of the
gullies.   Myriads of parrots shrieked and
chattered in the gum-trees, which grew almost
to the lake shore.   In many places, patches
of sand standing out in the water showed
how shallow the lake was, and told them
that in another month of drought it would
probably be quite dry, and that the mirage
might be seen.

CHAPTER XXIX.

'YOUR CHILDREN—OR ME!'

THE camp, a place which Tregaskiss had once dropped on by accident when out after stock, lay in the hollow of a rocky gully, to the west of the cone which, impracticable as it seemed at the first glance, was yet the easiest point where the range could be crossed. The gully was broken about halfway by a steep precipice, over which in rainy seasons there was a considerable fall of water. Now only a trickle made the tiniest cloud of spray upon a dark pool at the foot of the cliff. The pool, which was very deep, gave out a rivulet that watered a small plateau, well grassed, free from poison bush—the Western scourge—and closed in on three sides by the

range, thus forming a natural paddock, whence
cattle and horses could not easily stray.
Behind the waterfall was a good-sized cave,
and this it was settled should be turned into
the ladies' sleeping-room, a tarpaulin slung
across the entrance keeping out the spray—
though now this was hardly necessary—and
dry grass spread as a foundation for the
blankets. It was an enchanting nook, its
angle sheltered by the hills, its base debouch-
ing upon the low downs between the range
and the lake, while the breeze from the water,
caught as in a funnel, made it seem deliciously
cool after the long ride among scorched,
barren hills.

The riders had zigzagged down along
what was scarcely a track, over stones and
fallen logs, following Tregaskiss and the
black-boys, who were already dismounted
and hobbling their horses when the rest of
the party appeared. Ning, once off the
saddle, had forgotten her fatigue, and was
now running hither and thither, collecting
sticks for the fire, and helping the black-boys
to gather grass. The black-boys loved

Ning, and it was funny to hear her chatter-
ing to them in their own queer mixture of
English and blacks' language, and touching
to watch how careful they were not to let her
handle dead wood, or go where there was a
chance of her being bitten by a snake. The
gentlemen turned to—Geneste understood
how to bivouac—and very soon packs were
undone, horses watered and hobbled, a fire
blazing, the billies set on to boil, and the cave
got ready for the ladies to unpack and settle
their own belongings. Helen and the Cusack
girls, with Mrs. Tregaskiss, busied themselves
there, and Gladys Hilditch looked on with
deep interest while Shand and the Gulf man
cut two clean squares of bark, put on each a
heap of flour, and proceeded to mix and
knead damper and Johnny-cakes. Gladys
had declared that nothing would content her
but a true Bush picnic, and had insisted on
quart-pot tea and a damper. Geneste had
pleaded for Johnny-cakes, for which Shand
was noted, but the Gulf man swore by his
damper, and Gladys had appointed herself
umpire in the competition.

The sun had nearly reached the range opposite when the damper was ready for its bed of ashes. Ning shouted that the sea was in a blaze; and the blacks' fires, lower down the valley, seemed like sparks thrown out from the flaming trail across the lake. Ning wanted her mother to let her run along the gully till she came to the sandy shore. She would not believe that there was any possibility of her taking a wrong turn among the spurs below the plateau, and that so, getting out of sight of the water, she might, as Clare warned her, lose herself among the gum-trees. She wanted to look at the pelicans closer, to gather shells, to search among the black swans for the twelve white ones, who were, she said, the bewitched princes of Hans Andersen's story. And there were other things that she wanted more than to find the princes. To Ning, Lake Eungella was the scene of all the fairy stories. She had grown in that belief. It would have broken the heart of the imaginative child to be convinced that Andersen's people had no existence. Her mother read

her Andersen's stories every night, and Clare
herself had always a whimsical notion that
the scenes and people in them were real
scenes and real people somewhere.   Tregaskiss had started the theory by calling out,
when Ning asked her troublesome questions,
'Wunti?   Where?'—'Oh! over by Lake
Eungella, Pickaninny.' Unconsciously, Clare
had followed suit; and so Ning was firmly
persuaded that along the shores of Lake
Eungella lay all the wonderful countries of
storyland—the region in which the chimney-
sweep had wooed the proud princess; the
palace by the water, where the poor little
dumb mermaid had sat at the feet of the
prince; the Garden of Paradise; the Cave
of the Winds; and, Ning's ultimate desire,
the dwelling of that friendly witch who had
pulled in Gerda's boat, and petted her, and
made all the roses sink into the ground lest
they should remind her of Kay. Ning had
always felt indignant with Gerda for running
away from that delightful witch, with her
wonderful hat, her cherries, and her good
things, to whom little girls were so precious.

Ning had cherished the secret determination that she would find that old witch, and tell her how sorry she was for her loneliness, and that here was another little girl who really loved her, and who, though she might not leave Mummy and stay with her altogether, would come over as often as she could, and play in the beautiful garden, where the flowers told stories, and make up to her generally for the loss of Gerda. This determination, and these unselfish desires, Ning tried now to convey to her mother, who listened to the child's prattle with ears that hardly heard, and answered with lips which spoke mechanically. 'Oh, child, don't talk such nonsense; there's no such thing as Gerda's witch.'

Ning's great brown eyes stared at her mother in horrified reproof.

'Mummy, you been tell Ningie that Gerda's witch sit down alonga Lake Eungella. Mummy, ba'al you tell a lie. Mine thinks it that very wicked to tell a lie.'

'Yes, it's very wicked to tell a lie,' assented Clare wearily; 'but that isn't a lie. Gerda's

witch is only a story made out of a man's
head.'

'Mummy,' persisted Ning stolidly, 'you
been say that Gerda's witch sit down close
up Lake Eungella. Suppose not Lake
Eungella — where then?' Ning gave her
shoulders a queer little shrug, 'Wunti?'

'There's no such thing as Gerda's witch,'
repeated Clare.

Ning brooded for a minute.

'Mine not believe that,' she announced at
last; then, after another pause, 'Daddy been
tell Ning that Gerda's witch, and Hullaballoo,
and Blue-beard, and all the rest, sit down
alonga Lake Eungella. What for Daddy tell
a lie?'

'I don't know, Ning; go and ask him;
don't tease.'

'Mummy, mine certain sure Gerda's witch
sit down close up. Last night Ningie dream
—water like it this fellow water—rock like it
this fellow rock.' Ning waved her hand
dramatically. 'Mine see witches and garden
and little fellow house—that close up—over
there. I show you the place, Mummy.'

'No, Ning; dreams are nonsense.'

'In the Bible,' affirmed Ning, with triumphant conviction, 'dreams is true.' Presently — 'Mummy, will you come and find the witch?'

'No, Ning; I'm too tired.'

'Mummy, will you come and find the witch to-morrow?'

'I shall be too tired to-morrow; we've got to get home.'

'Mummy, you's always tired now. Ba'al you run about with Ning; ba'al tell Ning stories, or come and fish for craws or look out for chucky-chuckies. What for?'

'I'm getting old, child.'

'Then soon go bong, Mummy,' said Ning solemnly.

'Die,' corrected Clare; 'you mustn't talk blacks' language.'

'Suppose you go bong,' pursued Ning reflectively, 'then you go to heaven. There no witches sit down in heaven. Mummy'—persuasively—'come now and find Gerda's witch.'

'No; I'm too tired.'

'Mummy' — desperately — 'will you be tired in heaven ?'

'Oh, go away, child—go and find Auntie Gladys. Let Mummy think.'

'You's always thinking. Ning will think, too.'

The child put herself on a rock opposite her mother, crossed her little legs, put her arms round her knees as she had seen the stockmen and her father do, and, with a maddening pertinacity, fixed her solemn eyes upon her mother's face. In that attitude she had a curious resemblance to Tregaskiss.

'Go away, child; don't sit staring at me like that. Mummy has a headache; Mummy wants to be quiet.'

Ning got up very slowly and went away, throwing backward glances weighted with the purpose still in her mind.

'Daddy much gooder to Ning than Mummy,' she said. 'Daddy will take Ning to find Gerda's witch.' She paused for a minute, impishly daring. 'Daddy will let Ning go and find Gerda's witch,' she flung back, compromising with her conscience.

For Ning fully intended to find Gerda's witch, whether her father would or no; and when the prohibition did not come from her mother, as she expected, conceived herself free to act, and darted down to the lower camp-fire, where Tregaskiss and the little Cusacks and Miss Lawford had paused for a minute or two in their stroll down the valley, to have a patter with the black-boys.

To Clare Tregaskiss the child's importunate questioning had been but as the flutter round her head of some insistent winged thing, so absorbed was she in her own wretchedness, so beset by that reckless impulse to accept Geneste's offer, and to go away and be quit for ever of the burden of her marriage and its responsibilities. During that long ride she had worked herself into a mood in which the children's images seemed no more than blurs on a dull background of despair, and herself and Geneste the only living realities. It was a relief to have the child gone. She knew that Geneste was waiting till they could be alone to come and

talk to her; and she knew, too, that the
interview would be a momentous one.

She was sitting some distance from the
cave, in a sort of niche in the hilly wall which
bounded the plateau. Here the rocks seemed
to have been cloven by some ancient convul-
sion of the earth, and were bare and striated,
with broad ledges, forming a gentle tier of
natural benches. Upon one of these Clare
had placed herself. Projecting in front of
the niche, and scattered about the trough of
rock, were some granite boulders which
screened the hollow, so that no one at the
camps would have seen easily that she was
sitting there. She knew, however, that
Geneste had been watching her during her
stroll with Ning, and that he would come
and find her before many minutes had passed.
Her heart beat fast, and her bosom heaved
with an inward sob over her own pitiful condition. Her shoulder, where Tregaskiss had
struck her, ached dully beneath her linen
riding-jacket, and reminded her of her trouble.
She had not said a word to Geneste of the
scene with her husband—had, indeed, bidden

herself refrain from doing so; for all through
her resentment against Tregaskiss there was
the sense of having injured him, and a feeling
of justice which forced her to excuse him.
But now she did not seem able to bear
her suffering alone, and had the longing to
tell Geneste her sorrow, that a child might
have who seeks sympathy from its mother
after a blow.

The moon was not at its full, but was
shining brightly, and the night was so still
that every sound could be heard with great
distinctness, and seemed to send an echo
down from the narrow end of the gorge—
the clanking of the horses' hobbles and tinkle
of their bells; the noise of the black-boys at
their camp; the drip of the streamlet into
the pool; the gurgling sound of water-
reptiles; and at intervals the curlews' screech,
and the answering howl of dingoes.

Most of the party had wandered down
towards the lake, the gentlemen carrying
guns, Shand and the Gulf man on a business-
like expedition after pelicans, Tregaskiss and
Martin Cusack bound for a reedy water-hole

near the shore, where were numbers of wild-
duck.   Martin had gone on ahead, while
Tregaskiss dallied with Miss Lawford and
her young charges.   Helen had tried to
attach herself to the group, but they had
shown that she was not particularly welcome,
and Harold Gillespie, determined to say his
say, had drawn her off. Gladys and Blanchard
had disappeared.

Ning came upon her father at an inoppor-
tune moment.   She had run, shrieking her
request, after him, as he turned from the
black-boys' camp.

Tregaskiss only roared ' Stuff !' and ' Don't
let your Mummy make a goose of you, Pickaninny !' to Ning's tale of Gerda's witch. ' Go
back, and tell your Mummy to put you to
bed,' he shouted ; ' I don't want you ! It's
time for little girls, who have been on horseback all day, to go to sleep.'

Ning slunk back, wise enough to know
that persistence would call forth orders that
might not be disobeyed ; but after a minute
or two she followed the party some way
towards the more open country, a small

shadow in the moonlight, which was lost by-and-by among the gidia-trees.

Geneste had gone in search of Clare.

'Mrs. Tregaskiss,' said Geneste softly; then, as he came closer, 'Clare.'

He saw that she was alone. She turned upon him a white, tragic face, and made a little movement signifying that he might come beside her. He leaped, as well as his stiff leg would allow. across the mouth of the ravine, and into the shelter of the boulder against which she was leaning.

'Clare!' he repeated.

Still she did not speak, but stretched out her hand to his, and drew closer to him with a helpless gesture which touched him to the heart. He could hardly restrain the longing to fold her close in his arms, and soften and soothe her with loving caresses. He did, however, resist it, and only stroked and kissed the appealing hand.

'Something has happened?' he asked. 'I have seen it all day in your face. Why did you go off so suddenly to bed last night? I have been waiting and watching for a word.

in a perfect agony of anxiety, but you would scarcely look at me.'

'I couldn't,' she whispered.

'Clare,' he repeated, alarmed, 'it must be something very bad that has happened?'

'Is it? I don't know. At moments I feel wicked enough to be glad, for it seems to release me.'

His mind jumped at one conclusion, and yet was puzzled.

'Do you mean—you remember what I said —that you have a legal right to your freedom?'

'No, not that. I'm afraid to talk of it. I thought I wouldn't tell you, but I can't help it. Only, I beseech you, don't say anything to tempt me. You know what you said—that day riding to Ballandean. If you were to say it now, I might not be so strong as I was then. I might—fling everything up. I don't know what I mightn't do. I'm so lonely. Dear, I am so lonely!'

He could bear it no longer; she was in his arms, held fast and fiercely.

'No, don't,' she murmured, with an involuntary physical shrinking in the very

joy of his embrace. 'You hurt me.   I'm
bruised and sore.'

'Bruised?'   he   cried.   'How?   You
haven't had a fall?   Show me what it is.'

She   touched   her   shoulder,   withdrawing
herself.

'Never mind ; it does not matter.'

He said nothing, but quickly, and with a
doctor's deftness, unfastened the top of her
bodice,   and   the   white   neck,   with   that
purplish red mark reaching from shoulder to
chest, showed clearly in the moonlight.   The
cross on its thin gold chain, which she always
wore from a certain superstitious feeling of
reverence, showed, too, and reminded him of
her vow and of the barriers between them.
She looked at him, moved by the sudden
flaming of love and pity in his eyes, and by the
set, grim look of anger which intensified the
falcon expression of his face.   He examined
the bruise very gently, and then, with a
tenderness that set her sobbing, kissed the
place, as she herself might have kissed a
mark on her baby's soft flesh, before he closed
up the bodice again.

' He struck you ?'

'Yes.   He had been watching us—you
know——'

' But there was nothing——' Geneste
interrupted quickly.

' No ; it wasn't that.   He did not accuse
me.   He—I think he believes in me.   He—
oh, it's that is what makes me have a mad
longing to tear off the mask.   Can't you
understand ?'

' Oh, my poor Clare !   Yes, yes.   Tear it
off ; fling it away.   Isn't that what I am
begging of you ?'

' His grievance was senseless,' she went
on.   ' He said I was poisoning people's minds
against him—setting you against him —you—
and the child.'

' He was drunk, I suppose ?'

' Not that exactly ; he knew what he was
doing.'

' Oh !' exclaimed Geneste, with contempt.
' In a state of chronic alcoholism, it is not
so easy to make distinctions between
drunkenness and sobriety.   Well, surely this
ends it—for you ?'

'My married life is ended, certainly,' she answered in a dull tone.

There was silence for a few moments.

'What are you going to do?' he asked in a tone that purposely seemed indifferent in its quietude.

'Do? There's nothing for me to do,' she answered dully.

'Do you imagine that it will be possible for you to continue living under the same roof with your husband?' Geneste asked, this time showing emotion.

'What can I do? I have not a penny in the world. It's horrible!' she cried out. 'I told him that he made me hate him, and he said that he hated me; that I might go—to the devil, for all he cared.'

'Well, then, take him at his word; that is what I implore. Go—not to the devil, as he puts it, but to love, peace, happiness with me.'

Her face and attitude seemed to tell of the wavering impulses, the tottering rectitude which would not stand against too severe a strain.

She leaned back against the rock, her form drooping, her chin lowered, and a sound like a suppressed sob escaped her. He waited for a minute or two ; then, touching her hand in timid solicitude, said :

' Clare, tell me of what you are thinking.'

' If I did tell you,' she answered, ' I am afraid you would not altogether understand, and you would not sympathize with my feeling.'

' Try me. I cannot imagine any feeling of yours which could fail to command my fullest sympathy, even if it should tend against my own.'

' Not that. It is that my thoughts tend, in a way for which I can't quite account, to the side of my husband. You judge him too hardly.'

' Good heavens ! You don't mean that you find a justification for his conduct to you ?'

' No ; I know on the outside view of things he would be considered blameworthy. But I can't look upon our relation towards each other in the light of a debtor and creditor account. Through all my bitterness, and my dread and dislike of him, something in me pleads on his behalf. It's my sense of justice, I suppose.'

'Well,' he answered dryly, 'let me hear your pleadings. They should at any rate throw some light on the workings of your heart, and that must be valuable to us both. Things have come to a great crisis for us, Clare, and we must do our best to meet it fairly.'

'Oh, how can I balance rights and wrongs, and put down so much on his side of the case and so much on mine?' she flamed forth in emotional inconsistency. 'It seems to me as though I were penned in against a horrible black wall, over which the light only comes in dim flashes—a wall that's not of my own making, nor of his, but that's built by circumstance, tradition; or, say, by some fierce, inexorable Power which wanted to punish mankind for its sins, and so invented marriage!'

'You are wrong, dearest; there's nothing superhuman about your wall; it's of man's

building. Only resolution on your part is
needed to break it down, and you step forth
free to live your own life.'

'Ah! The wall has flesh and blood
buttresses. My little children——'

The catch in her throat stopped her. He
waited, and presently she recovered herself.

'I can't find any way out of it. It's hopeless—impossible. Don't you see? The
worst part of the tragedy is in our being just
simply what we were made—in our having
temperaments that are antagonistic to each
other. So that, to me, anyhow, the misfit is
an agony. In all our life together my nature
has been in secret antagonism with his. I
feel that, somehow, this has made a force
which has acted and reacted upon our real
selves, away from all the outside of things.
I don't know why I feel it, but it comes to
me continually. No matter how we try to
hide our thoughts and wishes, they go outside
of us and become something definite and
compelling which influences ourselves and
others. He has felt this antagonism, though
he couldn't reason about it, and though, in a

sense, he has trusted me.   I am guilty in
thought, even if——'

'Even if?' he repeated, not knowing how
to answer her.

'I was going to say even if I was not
guilty in act.   But I *am* guilty.   I am false
—false.   It isn't only the material sin.
There's the sin against the spirit, which
seems to hurt me more.   And, besides, I
can't help feeling that it was in the first
instance more my fault than Keith's.   I
ought never to have married him, knowing,
as in my heart I must have known, that I
did not truly love him.'

'That was indeed the terrible misfortune.
But it was circumstances that were to blame,
not you.'

'Yes, it was in a great measure circumstance ; and ignorance, and a false notion
altogether of life and of his character.
There's the awful cruelty of marriage.   The
forces bringing it about seem like so many
capricious winds driving us whither we know
not ; and often we are no more responsible
than autumn leaves whirled by chance

together. *Is* it all chance? Is it nothing but chance?' She gazed at him wildly. 'If I could believe it was only chance, and that there was no duty to anything higher——'

'Then?'

The eager entreaty in his voice had more force than a thousand casuistic arguments.

'I can't—I can't,' she murmured weakly.

'I think,' he said gently, 'that you take an exaggerated view of the thing. We have talked of this before; and it does not alter the facts of the situation. You are what you are; he is what he is. You can't be harmonized by Act of Parliament. And your children are half of him as well as half of you.'

'The children! Ah, dear Heaven! they are all that matters!'

What he said was pitilessly true. She remembered Ning's attitude and expression a little while before, and how it had reminded her of Tregaskiss. She remembered her revolt at different times against the beings she had brought into the world, because of those very traits and resemblances, which

declared that they were not wholly of her.
She could have loved her children passionately if they had been Geneste's. Was
she to blame because even Nature was in
conflict with the struggling maternal instinct,
so much less strong than the other instinct?
The ironic tragedy of the whole position came
over her with a force that shook her into
helpless sobs. Then Geneste seized his
opportunity. He put his arm round her and
drew her close to him. As she leaned her
head against his breast, it seemed to her that
she did not care for anything in the world
except the assurance of his deep affection.
There was now no more self-upbraiding; no
more entreaty; no more weighing of rights
and wrongs and of practical difficulties against
ideal joys. Everything seemed taken for
granted in the one convincing argument, 'We
were meant by fate for one another.'

It was getting late; the moon dipped below
mid-heaven. Coo-ees sounded in the gorge;
and the stray shots which they had heard,
unheeding, ceased. Now a very musical
'Coo-ee!' was sent forth quite near. Clare

knew it for the voice of Gladys, and started, reluctantly releasing herself from his arm. He still kept her hands when she rose.

'My dearest love! it is all settled now.'

The old struggle began once more.

'If it were not for the children—the poor little children!'

'*His* children!'

Geneste's manner changed. He stood before her, strong, masterful, and with his eyes fixed fiercely upon her face. The gaze seemed to force her to his will; she always felt that if he chose to look at her in that compelling way, she must do whatever he pleased. She had never in the case of any other human being experienced this sense of weakness.

'Clare,' he said, 'I am going to put you to the test. I feel that this is the crucial moment in your life and mine. It will never come again, and I don't mean to let it pass now. Your marriage, as such, you say is ended. You know what your life with me would be; you know what it must be for both apart. You know, too, the misery of the half-union—the beating against bars you put up between us, the pretence of obedience in keeping away from you, and the misery it has caused us these past weeks. We can't live like that; it must be one thing or the other. Choose—now, to-night.'

'Choose?' she repeated faintly.

'You must choose between your children and me—that's what it all comes to. I leave your husband out of the question; you owe him nothing. It is your children — *his* children or me.'

'You will leave me?' she asked.

'I have made up my mind to end the strain one way or the other, because I see that the situation is impossible. If you refuse me I shall go away from you for ever. I shall suffer cruelly for months, years —you know that such a blow must alter the whole current of a man's life. But other men have had to bear such blows, and have lived on like other men, and got to be happy even—in time. I am only "just a man," as you say.' His voice had a bitterness of which she was very conscious. 'I don't profess to have superhuman strength any more than superhuman virtue. The wound will always be there, but after years it will become cauterized, and I shall get strong.'

'Oh, you are strong now—horribly strong.'

'I shall get over it; one can endure the inevitable. You see, I am taking the selfish view. I do so on purpose. As for you, you will die if you go on here—die before many years are past, and be to me only a memory and a grave. It will be better for you to die than to live on this kind of life. I have already put this before you.'

'I know it. I shall die, perhaps like poor Mrs. Carmody—why do I call her "poor," I wonder?—but I shall not be glad as she was when she was dying, that she had done her duty.'

'No, you will not be glad. You will feel that you have sacrificed your own life and happiness as well as my welfare for nothing. But you won't do that, Clare.' His whole manner changed again from its deliberately dictatorial tone, and again his voice became exceedingly tender. 'You won't do that?'

'What do you want me to do?'

The words came from her as if forced by torture.

'I want you never to go home again. I want you to ride with me, when we leave this place, straight away to Port Victoria, where we can catch the boat to Sydney; and I want you to have done with your old life for ever. You will do this? Don't worry over small details and obstacles. Everything is arranged.'

'You had planned this?'

'Yes—deliberately. I own it. I looked out the steamers before we left Darra this morning — after I had seen your face at breakfast. I have spoken, too, to Ambrose Blanchard, and he has agreed, in case of my being called away suddenly, to undertake the management of Darra. We shall ride on ahead when we start on the home journey, and turn off by a short-cut that I know to a Bush inn, where I have saddle-horses in the paddock. By pushing forward we shall catch the evening train to Port Victoria, and the boat South, almost before they realize here that we have gone.'

The coolness and audacity of his plan were as a new force suddenly turned upon her, impossible to fight against. There was no resistance in her feeble protest.

'And if I do not go?'

'Then I shall. I am quite resolved, for your sake as well as my own. I cannot live in your neighbourhood knowing what your life is, and knowing that I have no power to help you. You could not bear it, either; it would kill you and embitter me. I shall go as far away as I can from you, and try to blot this year out of my life—as much as it is possible for me to do so.'

Again the coo-ee sounded, and Gladys' voice called 'Clare!'

Mrs. Tregaskiss moved from the boulder.

'I must go.'

'Not till you have given me your answer. I *must* know. It is life union or utter separation from to-night. Clare, which is it to be?'

He took her two hands, and they stood

for several moments, the two pairs of eyes gazing into each other. Hers quailed ; her arms went up round his neck.

'I love you,' she said.

'You will come ?'

'Yes, I will come.'

'Oh, I will never let you regret it, my love—my wife.'

'Now I am going,' she said. 'I have given you your answer ; you should be content. From this moment I shall be a different woman—not the old Clare Tregaskiss any more. I will not hear Ning say her prayers to-night. To-morrow she will have no mother.'

'Do not fear for her, Clare. If you believe in Heaven's providence, you should believe that she will be cared for.'

Clare shuddered. 'What mockery ! Do I believe in Heaven ? Don't you know that I am disobeying the laws of my Church ? It is better for me not to believe in Heaven's providence.'

'Clare, is it a pledge ? You won't change ?'

'I won't change, and it is a pledge. Look here.' She fumbled at her neck and drew out the chain and cross. 'You know what I swore upon this; it was a false oath. If I believed in Heaven, I should believe that punishment would come upon me through my children. See what I am defying—for you. I've broken my oath—for love of *you*. I have no use for this any longer.'

She tore apart the fastening of the chain and flung the cross, with all the strength of her arm, out into the ravine. They saw it bound against a rock, take a fresh impetus and bound again, disappearing in the cleft where no search would ever again bring it to light. Then Clare spoke solemnly:

'It was my mother's cross. I swore upon it by my children that I would be true to my duty. Now my oath is broken. I am a wicked woman, and I don't care—I don't care—because I love you.'

CHAPTER XXX.

OUTSIDE THE CAVE.

Mrs. HILDITCH was standing not far from the boulders when Clare emerged from the cleft, in advance of Geneste. He and she both had the feeling of being detected criminals. The humiliation was horrible, and made Clare more recklessly determined to fling off falsities. Gladys had scented the situation, and Clare's face confirmed her suspicions. She knew that there had been a critical love-scene—guessed that Geneste had persuaded Clare to run away with him. Gladys was so happy herself that her whole being throbbed in sympathy with love, even though it might be of an illegitimate kind. She felt a guilty spasm of joy at the thought

that Clare had determined to take the law
into her own hands, and then was frightened
at herself for being glad. Gladys resolved
to fight as far as she could on the side of
conventionality and the children. 'Ah, the
children ! That was just all that mattered,'
Gladys said to herself, too.

'Clare,' she whispered, 'I have been
looking for you. I am afraid Mr. Tregaskiss is angry at your being out so long;
they've all come back. Helen and Miss
Lawford have gone to bed, and I let Mr.
Tregaskiss think that you were in the cave,
too.'

'That was very devoted of you, Gladys—
to tell a lie for my sake,' Clare answered in
an odd tone. 'But I think we'll undeceive
Keith now; we are not going to have any
more lies after to-night.'

'Clare, do you mean——'

At that moment Geneste came up to them,
and said in his self-possessed manner :

'I'm afraid it is very late, Mrs. Hilditch,
and the fault is mine of keeping Mrs. Tregaskiss out. It is a lovely moonlight night,

isn't it? I think I had better go to my camp now; and I hope you ladies won't find the cave very uncomfortable. Good-night!'

He shook hands formally with Gladys, but did not say anything to Clare.

To Gladys the omission was significant; to Clare, a recognition on his part of their new relation towards each other, and of her declaration that there were to be no more lies. He walked away in the direction of one of the camp-fires—the furthest—where Blanchard and Martin Cusack were sitting. Close by, the black-boys lay wrapped in their blankets, having heaped their smouldering log with twigs to make a smoke against the mosquitoes. The horses had got as near the smoke, too, as they dared, and were whisking their tails and making the bells round their necks jingle as they jerked their heads. Beside the fire, nearest the cave, Tregaskiss, Shand, and the Gulf man were lounging, their pipes alight, their guns at their feet, and two or three dead pelicans and several brace of wild-duck on the ground outside the

tent. They were talking noisily, discussing
the evening's sport, and Clare, as she walked
close by, heard Tregaskiss say :

'By Jove! I'm sorry now I didn't let the
pickaninny come ; it would have been a
regular adventure for her, and would have
cleared her head of that witch rubbish. She's
kept too much at home, and stuffed with fairy-
tales and rot. I'm not going to have it any
longer ; she shall ride about with me, and, my
word ! she'll soon be sitting a buck-jumper.
There's not a seat on the Leura can beat
hers.'

'Where's Ning, Mr. Tregaskiss ?' Gladys
called out, not for the sake of information,
but as something to say that he might know
they were near.

Tregaskiss looked up and saw his wife.
His face flushed with anger.

'So it's you at last !' he growled, with scant
ceremony. 'I guessed you weren't in the
cave. About time, isn't it ? for decent folks
to come in and go to bed. I sent Ning hours
ago, but I suppose her mother was too well
occupied to see after her.'

'Ning always puts herself to bed, you know,' cheerfully observed Gladys.

'And her mother hears her say her prayers,' sneered Tregaskiss. 'The prayers went to the wall to-night. I hate damned hypocrisy.'

'Can't I do anything for you, Mrs. Tregaskiss?' cried Shand, coming forward and trying to create a diversion in his usual clumsy fashion. 'I beg your pardon; I didn't see you. Look at our bag! Those pelican-skins are going to be cured for trimming a dress or cloak or something for Ning; it's awfully like grebe, isn't it? Oh yes! the mosquito-nets are slung up, Mrs. Hilditch; and I do hope you won't get much bitten. Good-night! Sure I can't do anything?' And he left them in front of the tarpaulin which protected the entrance to the cave, having, as Gladys gratefully observed, covered their retreat.

Mrs. Tregaskiss pushed aside the tarpaulin. No light but that of the moon was in the cave, but it was sufficient to show the row of forms stretched on narrow beds of heaped

grass and leaves, over which waterproof sheet-
ing and blankets had been spread, though
the features of the sleepers could not be dis-
tinguished. She purposely avoided looking
at the furthest recess, which, being partially
screened by a projecting piece of rock, had
been arranged by Geneste for Clare and
Ning. It seemed impossible to Clare that
she could spend the rest of that night by her
child's side—the child whom she had for-
sworn an hour ago, and whom she would
desert on the morrow. Some tender impulse clutched at the mother's heart then,
but she shook herself free from the thought
of those helpless babes, taking refuge in that
of her pledge to Geneste. She would force
herself to keep it; she would not expose
herself to the chance of another conflict of
emotions; she would abstain as far as she
could from looking into her child's face.

She stooped and picked up a waterproof
that lay near the tarpaulin curtain.

' I'm not going to sleep in there,' she said ;
' it's too stifling. I shall lie down on the rock
outside.'

Gladys tried to dissuade her.

'Ning might wake and be frightened,' she urged.

'There will be plenty of people to comfort her,' said the mother, still in that odd voice.

Gladys took a blanket from her own couch, which was the nearest the entrance.

'Well, you shall have this to lie upon. Come, and we'll find a cosy place; but, oh, the mosquitoes! You will be eaten alive and made hideous, which is a consideration that would certainly appeal to me.'

'I'll tie my veil round my face,' said Clare; and Gladys gave way, remarking that she supposed snakes were as likely to be inside the cave as out.

They found a hollow on the waterfall platform, sheltered on two sides, and with a rocky floor. Gladys spread the blanket, and went back for an armful of leaves and grass. Clare sat down; she would not lie, saying she was not sleepy.

'Neither am I. And I've got something

to tell you. I want you to know that I am very happy.'

' I know that already, Gladys.'

' Oh, you couldn't help knowing. It's in my very self, and comes out at the pores of my skin.'

' And from your eyes, and in your laugh, and in the tone of your voice—since yesterday,' said Clare.

' Ah! I only knew for certain last night. I don't deserve it. I've been so bad. I'm not worthy of him. But that's the beauty of love, Clare. It—it's like the salvation through Christ. Don't think me irreverent, dear. I solemnly mean it. Nothing matters —not even badness, for love washes it all away. Oh, my dear, dear friend, nothing matters but love, and money is of no account whatever.'

' You'll lose your money. Oh no—I quite agree with you. That is not of the least consequence—if the love lasts.'

' It will last ; it has lasted without a shadow of change—in me, anyhow, since the first moment I saw him. And I was married then, and I suppose it was wicked of me to care for him. Well, I couldn't help it. And through all that time of misery and humiliation and loneliness, I knew that my only hope lay in him. That was why I came out. I *meant* to make him marry me!'

'And you have succeeded?'

'Not quite yet; but he won't break his word now that he has given it. I had to make him ask me. He fought hard against it. It was all my wretched money and his pride; and to-night we fought a battle to the death over it, and I killed his pride, and he had to acknowledge himself conquered.'

Clare pressed her friend's hand, but made no response. Gladys knew why she could not speak, and went on :

'Of course we shall be dreadfully poor; but I shall get him to England, and then things will come right with his father. And I shall wait and save—I don't mind cheating Mr. Hilditch's heirs that way. And I've got a balance of nearly £2,000; and we shall manage somehow—and I mustn't buy any more lace or fripperies. Clare

darling, I want to thank you—to thank you
with all my heart for having me here, and
giving me the chance of getting near to
him and of finding out that he did love me,
after all.'

The women kissed each other.

'Clare,' whispered Gladys—'oh, my poor
dear, I'm so sorry for you!'

'There's no need.'

'Yes, there is. Do you think I don't
know? You and I have been bound by the
same chain; we've suffered in the same way,
and we both know the hideousness of it.
Clare, there's nothing in the whole universe
so good as love; and there's nothing in the
world so immoral as living with a man you
can't care for, when you love another man.
Listen. If you were going away with Dr.
Geneste to-morrow, if it wasn't for the children, I'd say you were doing right.'

'And the children?'

Clare spoke as quietly as though the affair
concerned another person; only the twitch in
her eye betrayed her emotion. She admitted
nothing. Gladys knew that she would not

acknowledge her intention, but none the less was Gladys sure of it.

'The children make the wrong. Oh, it would be a crime, a cruelty, to leave them! Clare, you are not intending *that?*'

Clare made no reply.

'Think!' pleaded Gladys. 'He would marry again. Think of poor little Ning and the baby! And a stepmother—or worse.'

Clare shuddered, but still said nothing.

'Clare!' cried Gladys desperately. 'You won't speak; you will tell me nothing. You are stone outside; but do you think I don't know that you are suffering tortures?'

'I *am* suffering tortures. I want to end them.'

'Oh, how can you fancy that you will end them by running away! The children will haunt you to your life's end.'

Still silence. Gladys went on:

'Take them with you. Go, and live your own life; you are justified, if you go alone. But, oh! wait to live that other love-life. Wait, anyhow, a few months—a few years. You don't know what may happen. Some-

thing, perhaps, which would put you in the
right and give you freedom. Don't put yourself in the wrong first. Go away, if you like,
but alone with the children.'

'You forget that I have no money to live
an independent life with.'

'What does that matter? I have enough
to help you.'

'You forget, too,' said Clare slowly, 'that
they are my husband's children, and that
I have not the right to take them away from
him.'

Gladys made an impatient gesture.

'He would not dare to go to law.'

'I can't enter into that. I suppose there's
such a thing as moral right, and, bad as I
may be in some ways, I feel the justice of
that. He loves Ning better than I do.
What is natural instinct with him, is—has
been—only duty with me. Gladys,' she
added, 'don't let us speak of that any more.
You are a good woman and a true friend, and
I thank you with my whole heart. But you
can't judge for me. I must choose my own
path, and go where it leads me.'

She got up, as she spoke, from her leaning posture ; it was a sign of dismissal. Gladys was not perhaps altogether sorry that, for the time, she must close the discussion. Clare had shut herself up in a chamber of reserve, to which she could not penetrate. Gladys knew that Clare must be meditating some decisive step—guessed, indeed, what the step was—but had no idea that it was likely to be put immediately into execution. She could not run away with Dr. Geneste that night, at any rate ; and Gladys was herself so physically weary, as well as so utterly happy in the glow of her new understanding with Blanchard, that she longed for rest, and for the silent watches, in which she might assure herself of the reality of her joy.

'I see that you are tired out,' said Mrs. Tregaskiss. 'Go and sleep.'

'I shall not sleep, but of course I am tired. You must be tired, too, Clare. Won't you come and lie down beside Ning ?'

'No ; I am better here.'

'Are you going to stay here all night ?'

'Perhaps.   But the morning can't be so very far off.'

'I don't like to leave you, Clare.'

'Why not ?   It is my mania to enjoy being alone.   Don't trouble about me.   Go and rejoice, as I do, dear, too, in your happiness. Perhaps I shall be happy as well, some day— or when I'm dead, like poor Mrs. Carmody. She did her duty, and minded her children. And what was the use of it all ?   Duty doesn't pay on the Leura.   Good-night, Gladys.'

'Good-night, Clare.'

They kissed again.   Gladys was turning away, but Clare stopped her for a moment.

'I have never pretended to be a good mother, and you must take that into account. But I have done my best, and I have always been dreadfully sorry for the poor little children.   Oh! there's something horrible,' she cried, 'in their having to come into the world whether they choose or no—the fruit of a marriage that's not the sacramental marriage we used to talk of in the old days. Oh, how different that would make it all !

Do you remember, dear, how we used to say to each other that we'd choose the highest—or nothing? Instead of that, we both chose the lowest. Now we have found out our mistake; but you have been able to mend yours, and I haven't.'

'You will—some day. You'll be happy, as I am, some day—able to be with *him*.'

'Perhaps. Yes, probably I shall be with him some day. But that doesn't alter the fact that the poor little children were brought wrongly into the world. They are children of sin and shame—worse off than if—— For when they've come through love, their mother must have a different feeling for them; and that's just the wrong in me. Well, I suppose God knows all about it. He should care for them, and put the wrong right, and raise friends for them better than their wicked mothers. Gladys, I just wanted to ask you to think of that, when—when you've got children of your own. I just wanted to say —if anything should happen to me, and it ever comes in your way—you'll be kind, won't you, to my Ning and Baby?'

CHAPTER XXXI.

THE PENALTY.

THROUGH the hours Clare Tregaskiss remained half lying, half crouching in the hollow beside the cave. She had in a mechanical fashion prepared herself for the night, piling up against the wall of rock the leaves and grass Gladys had brought, thus making a sort of cushion, upon which she reclined, her waterproof spread over it, and the blanket covering her knees. The mosquitoes, having scant shelter of herbage just here, were not so troublesome as down on the grassy plateau, or perhaps she did not feel them. Anyhow, she untied the veil she had fastened round her head and face, and stayed during the night bareheaded, and with wide eyes staring out over the desolate Bush.

The scene harmonized with her mood. It was her impulse always when she was wretched or torn by rebellious longings to make for the wildest and loneliest spot she could find. To-night she was so physically exhausted, and so wrought up mentally, that she was barely conscious of material facts. She had a gruesome fancy of herself as of one walking on the edge of a precipice, the pledge to Geneste her foothold, as it were; the thought of her children and of the life she was going to give up typified in the black vacuum below, from which to save herself she must keep away her eyes and her mind, but which was always horribly present. Everything else was a confusion of sounds and dim images, except the light of Geneste's camp, and the thrilling consciousness of that steel-like, invisible chain binding their two beings together. Sometimes Ning's solemn dark eyes would shine out of the gulf, and then she would wince and totter, and in terror draw herself together and turn her own eyes inward.   Sometimes she would fancy that she heard Ning's voice, in its quaint, half-aboriginal utterance, raised in accents of pain and distress, and at such moments would have difficulty in assuring herself that on the other side of the rocky wall Ning lay soundly sleeping.

It was not strange that uncanny fancies should visit her, for the ghostly scene and the night sounds were enough to make stout nerves creep.   The Bush was full of gurglings and rustlings ; and a sense of mystery and of the illimitable seemed to breathe from the desolate stretches, the moon-made shadows, the straight, bare stems of the gum-trees, the dark clumps of gidia, and the gray upheaved boulders.   The 'hop-hop' of wallabies came from among the fallen timber in the gorge behind her ; there was the shrill chirrup of the tree-frog, and there were throaty noises from nameless reptiles making for the pool below the cave.   Here some white-barked crooked trees bent like ghosts over the water, upon whose inky blackness the moon cast a feeble ray, giving a new touch of

dread to the scene. She could hear the
heavy flapping of flying foxes' wings, and
from the scrub came the dismal howling of
dingoes, and, nearer, the curlew's wail. That
sound, which for a second she fancied to be
Ning's voice calling ' Mummy !' was from the
native bear, which has a cry like a little child.
The moon went slowly down, and by-and-by
she must have slept a little, for she awoke to
see that faint grayness on the edge of the
sky which heralds dawn, and to hear the
more-pork giving its early note, and the long,
derisive chuckle of the laughing jackass.

She watched the day break, heard the
rousing of the black-boys when they went
after the horses, and then, stiff and aching,
got up and stole round to the entrance of the
cave. She fancied they might think it strange
that she should have been out all night, and
thought that she would lie down and make a
pretence of having come in and slept like the
rest. But the unconquerable dread she had
of meeting Ning's eyes, and of hearing the
child's prattle, held her back, and instead
she went down to the rocks and to a lonely

pool, an outlet of the larger pool, where she washed and did her hair, and got rid of some of the traces of her vigil. The sun was quite up by the time she had finished, and she was mounting the rocks again, when she heard a call from the cave, 'Ning! Ning!' and then her own name in Gladys' voice, 'Clare!'

She quickened her steps. Gladys met her before she reached the cave; the tarpaulin was drawn back, and Helen Cusack and her sisters stood before the entrance. Clare, in her dazed way, noticed that they looked alarmed.

'Have you got Ning with you?' Gladys asked.

She spoke sharply, and her eyes had a frightened expression.

'Ning?' cried Mrs. Tregaskiss, startled. 'No, I have not seen her. Is she not in the cave?'

'We can't find her,' answered Gladys. 'I thought you might have come in when we were asleep, and taken her out.'

'She is in bed,' said Clare, turning white with an undefined fear.

'I don't believe she has been in bed all night,' cried Gladys. 'The blanket looks as if it had never been disturbed. There was a roll of waterproofs and things on it, and that made me think she was there. It was so dark in the cave, and I never looked closely.'

The Cusack children joined in. They had been so tired that they had tumbled into bed without thinking of Ning. Miss Lawford spoke of the child having begged her father to look for Gerda's witch with her, and of how he had sent her back to bed. Not one of them had seen Ning since then. There were no traces of her in the cave. The obvious inference was that she had never been back.

As she listened, blackness came over Clare —the blackness of the inn at Cedar Hill, when she had awakened to the sight of Geneste. She tottered against the rock, and her blood seemed to rush away from her body. In a few seconds the blackness passed, and her heart beat quickly, and a tingling came into her limbs as the blood

flowed again. Gladys was supporting her,
and Helen was at her other side. By a kind
of divination, she knew that some awful thing
had occurred, and that she had called down
a doom upon her child. Gladys and Helen
heard her say in a terrible sort of inward
whisper, 'God has punished me! He has
killed Ning!'

'Oh, Mrs. Tregaskiss! don't be frightened.
It's sure to be all right, and I expect she is
just playing round,' said Helen; 'or perhaps
she has gone to one of the other camps. I'll
run and see.'

Helen flew to the nearest of the camps,
where Tregaskiss, just risen from his blankets,
was rating a black-boy for having let one of
the horses stray. Shand, the Gulf man, and
Martin Cusack were kindling the fire, and
making preparations for the baking of Johnny-
cakes, while Geneste and Blanchard were
filling the billies with water.

'Ning? My good God! she's gone stray-
ing, and has lost herself!' cried Tregaskiss,
horror-stricken, when Helen told him how
the child was missing. 'I sent her back to

bed when we went shooting last night. I haven't seen her since.'

It was the same story with all. No one had beheld Ning since she had called after her father, and he had told her it was time for pickaninnies to be asleep. Everybody who had thought about her at all had supposed that she had put herself to bed as was her habit at home. Those who had thought of her upon going into the cave, seeing, in the dim moonlight, the bundle upon her blankets in the recess, had imagined it to be Ning herself coiled up in profound slumber. Besides, they had, of course, expected that her mother would be beside her. When Tregaskiss learned that Clare had not slept in the cave, his mad anger knew no bounds. He uttered words which were not pleasant for bystanders to hear.

Meanwhile, the gorge rang with 'coo-ees' and calls of 'Ning! Ning!' Miss Lawford, glad to escape from the scene between Tregaskiss and his wife, rushed about with the Cusack girls, peering into impossible crannies. Helen and Martin searched more systematically round the plateau. Clare herself was like one upon whom a doom had fallen, and who knows there is no use in resistance. She bore her husband's reproaches with perfect quietness, not stirring a muscle, still and stony, as though the nerves of hearing had been paralyzed.

'Have you no feeling at all, that you stand there like a marble statue?' roared Tregaskiss, who had completely lost his head. 'By God! if anything has happened to the Pickaninny through your neglect, I'll never speak to you or look on your face again. As for me, I'd as soon be dead and done for as lose the Pickaninny.'

Geneste and Blanchard stepped up to him. Ambrose spoke first.

'Look here, Mr. Tregaskiss; it isn't as bad as that, and this isn't the way to take it. Mrs. Tregaskiss is no more to blame than you or I, or any of us. The child will be found again all right, you may be certain. She has just strayed and lost herself, and we've got to lose no time in looking for her. Let's settle at once what to do.'

'We had better divide into search-parties,' said Geneste. 'Each one take a black-boy, except, perhaps, myself and Martin Cusack. He's a good tracker, and I'm used to it.'

'I'll back Geneste to track a flitter across running water,' cried the Gulf man.

Tregaskiss bestirred himself with feverish activity. Geneste took command, and presently the horses were saddled, and the search-parties started, Tregaskiss foremost. Soon every human being of that pleasure-seeking expedition was scouring range, gullies, flats, and lake-shore for little Ning.

The ladies of the party and the new-chums kept near the gorge, and searched the ground, going in line, to and fro, among the gullies, shouting as they went; but no answering call came, and there was no sign of the child. Then they went towards the lake, but of no avail. At one o'clock a black-boy among the searchers struck a track, for about ten yards, on the old Eungella road, and then again, for about a hundred yards, on a cattle-path—just two tiny boot-marks—but it was lost again completely. The tracks ran inland

from the lake, and were a long way from the
camp, telling a pathetic tale of the poor baby's
night wanderings.   They made these tracks
the point of a fresh start in all the directions
round.   Blanchard rode back with the news ;
and Gladys and Helen, and even Miss Lawford, wept with joy, for now they felt sure Ning
would be found.   But Clare did not shed a
tear or give a smile ; nor did she show any
anxiety in putting together food, and a blanket
in which to wrap the child when they should
come upon her.   She had been walking
aimlessly, her face a mask of despair—walking because she could not sit still, not with
any hope.

'I know that Ning is dead,' she said, in
her stony voice.   'There is no use in taking
food ; she will not need it.   But I should
like to have her little dead body, so that the
dingoes and wild-birds may not hurt it.'

Her calmness was terrible ; she did not
shudder, like the rest, at the horrible suggestion.

'Ambrose, I think she is going mad,'
whispered Gladys.   'She never says a word ;

only walks—walks—with that awful set face.
What can we do ?'

'We will bring the child, please God!
before many hours are over ; and all that we
can do is to search,' he answered. 'If only
there were a station near, where we could
get search hands and fresh horses. There
are so few of us. Geneste is tracking like a
black fellow or a Red Indian, and Tregaskiss
will not let the black-boys stop for a moment,
though he is so wild with grief that he is not
much use in himself. The child *must* be
saved, if it is humanly possible to save her.'

He rode away again, and there were more
interminable hours of waiting. All they
could do still was to wander, and shout, and
make fires on the hills, which should attract
the little creature, if she were hidden in one
of the ravines near. No one came back that
night from the outside searchers. The night
was passed in that aimless wandering, and in
broken snatches of sleep taken in relays, the
watchers starting at cries of curlews or
native bear, in the fancy that it might be the
voice of the child. The country blazed with

the fires they had lighted; and some went
down to the lake shore, the distraught mother
among them, and covered miles walking
along the sand.   But there was no Ning.

In the morning, after the second night,
Tregaskiss crawled up to the camp, lame, his
feet cut by the stones through his boots, his
hands bleeding, and his eyes wild and blood-
shot.   He had been tracking on foot by
moonlight, and had lost himself, till he had
been able to strike the gorge at daybreak.
Now he had come for one of the ladies'
horses, for those they had were knocking up.
Clare was still wandering by the lake shore,
and perhaps it was well that she did not see
her husband, for her heart would only have
been harrowed the more.   Helen and Miss
Lawford brought him some damper and beef,
and he ate it mechanically, taking no notice
of either of them in words, but Helen fancied
that he turned away from Miss Lawford with
something like a shudder.   He was curiously
subdued, and there was an expression upon
his face, in all its wildness, almost solemniz-
ing—a faint reflection of that look which

Paul of Tarsus must have worn when he came back to Damascus blind. What had been his thoughts during those lonely hours no one knew; but Gladys partly guessed them. He came up to her while they were catching and saddling Helen's horse.

'I don't want to see my wife,' he said; 'but you can tell her I am sorry that I spoke to her as I did. I am as much to blame as she is for Ning's death. Yes, Mrs. Hilditch, Ning is dead.' He fixed his eyes with their strange spiritualized expression on Gladys' face, and she wondered if this were in truth the old Tregaskiss; his features seemed to have so curiously sharpened and all his bloated look and coarseness to have disappeared. 'She came to me last night out in the Bush,' he went on. 'I saw her as plain as I see you. She stood in front of me, and held out her little arms, and then she vanished. She held out her little arms,' he repeated huskily. 'She was always fond of her Daddy—the Pickaninny——' His voice broke altogether, and the great fellow gave a choking cry, and, flinging himself forward with his head upon his arms, heaved and shook in an agony of uncontrollable grief. 'I—I—can't bear it!' he sobbed. 'I doted —on the Pickaninny!'

Gladys sobbed too; it was as much at the sight of his grief as for the Pickaninny. He looked utterly broken, and she guessed that the enforced abstinence from stimulant of so many hours had something to do with his shattered condition. She brought him some brandy, but, to her great surprise, he took the pannikin and dashed it to the ground.

'No more of that for me!' he cried. 'I've drunk my last drop of grog, and I'm done for ever with it; and with other things, too. Something came over me last night, Mrs. Hilditch, that has made a changed man of me.'

Gladys wondered, but she did not speak. Tregaskiss got up and shouted with one of his old oaths to the black-boy to be quick with the horse.

'She's dead!' he murmured; 'but I've got to find her. It kills me to think of my Pickaninny's pretty face — and perhaps the dingoes——' Again he gave a great sob, and his hand and arm shook as he drew the reins tight in order to mount. 'You may tell Clare,' he said, bending down, 'that I'm a changed man. Before Heaven, I mean it.'

CHAPTER XXXII.

GLADYS had a good cry to herself. She told Helen Cusack what had happened, and the two looked for Clare, who was walking along the shore of the lake in a dreary, mechanical way, with a fixed, vacant stare on the ground, which showed plainly that she had given up all hope, if, indeed, she had ever had any.

Later on, Helen came upon Miss Lawford, lying, her face to the ground, in passionate tears. Ambrose Blanchard rode into camp in the afternoon, faint, worn and dispirited. The tracks had come to nothing, and there was still no trace of the child. He had been searching during the night as long as the moon lasted, and the others had gone forth again ; but now all were becoming hopeless, and they had no expectation of finding Ning alive. Geneste, he said, had more than once struck tracks, but had lost them again. He had never stopped to sleep, eat or rest. Fortunately they had met with a party of fencers, and had been able to get two fresh horses and more hands. One of the fencers had gone to give the alarm at the Bush township of Eungella, and to call out the police. Ambrose came now to see how the ladies and the new-chum in charge of them were getting on for provisions, and to con-sult as to the advisability of their making for Darra-Darra. They, too, were becoming worn out, and Gladys was deeply alarmed for Clare, who kept always the same marble face, and did nothing but walk in that mechanical, chained - beast fashion. She would not hear, however, of leaving the place.

' I know that Ning is dead !' she repeated ; 'but I will not go away till they have buried her.'

Her composure was that of a madwoman,

and Blanchard got frightened also. Gladys
was fretted to a shadow, but held out bravely,
and smiled at him radiantly. Happiness is
an effective spur to heroism. Helen, too,
though her pretty freshness had gone, was
self-collected and grandly devoted, taking
turns with Gladys to watch, if from a distance, poor distracted Clare. It was hysterical
little Miss Lawford who showed want of
courage. She wept profusely, and wildly
entreated to be taken home. What was the
use of her staying? She could do no good
to poor little Ning. She was dying of
terror; and she knew that Mr. Tregaskiss
had turned against her and blamed her for
the loss of the child. She had done nothing,
she declared, to be treated so. Mrs. Cusack
would be uneasy, too, about the children;
and what was to hinder their being murdered
by blacks in that lonely, unprotected camp!
Might they not have a black-boy, or one of
the gentlemen who knew the way, and be
taken to Darra-Darra?

'You know, the black-boys are more
valuable than any of us as trackers,' said

Blanchard. 'I wish to Heaven we could spare somebody,' he added in an aside to Helen, 'and get rid of her!'

Whereupon Helen, roused to gentle wrath, rebuked the governess so sternly for her selfish want of consideration that Miss Lawford retired abashed, shrieking that no one knew what she was suffering and how her heart was broken, and hid herself in the cave, where she gave way to a prolonged bout of sobbing. By what she called afterwards a 'miraculous coincidence,' deliverance came just after Blanchard had gone, in the shape of her old admirer the Land Commissioner, who, having heard the sad news from the fencer on his way to Eungella, had left the men with him to help in the search, and at Geneste's instance had hurried on to the camp.

Gillespie came with the Commissioner; he was not a good enough Bushman to be of great service to the seekers, and not in health for continued exertion and hardship. He had a word of good news. Two black-boys from Eungella, who were noted trackers, had

joined the party; they had found a clue in
the shape of some of Ning's garments and
one little boot; and it was probable that the
end was now near.

The Land Commissioner saw his opportunity, and seized it. Woebegone and
dishevelled as she was, Miss Lawford seemed
to him more attractive in her pleading helplessness than when confident and tricked out
in her showy finery. He was moved to the
heart by the way in which she clung to him.
He was a good Bushman, and knew the road,
and there was no reason why he should not
escort her and the two Cusack girls to Darra-
Darra at once. Helen indignantly refused to
accompany them; but, though Minnie and
Dollie rebelled, and protested that it was
cowardly to leave the others in their distress,
this was obviously the wisest course, and so
the Commissioner had the horses saddled,
and the four rode away, to the relief of those
who remained.

That afternoon Nature asserted herself
Clare fainted in her restless tramp, and
was for a long time unconscious. About

sundown the thud of horses' feet sounded in
the gorge, and one by one, winding down
the range, a straggling line of riders appeared.
Geneste, torn, unshaven, bent, having become, as it were, an old man in those three
days, was foremost. He carried no burden.
There was not a 'Coo-ee' uttered, and the
silence and his miserable face told Helen,
who saw them first, only too surely that the
search was ended, and that Ning would
never come back again.

She ran to meet him. She was practically
alone in the camp, for Clare Tregaskiss was
lying in a half-stupor in the cave, with Gladys
watching her, and Harold Gillespie had gone
upon a last despairing hunt in the crannies of
the gorge.

Geneste dismounted at the foot of the
rock, and tried to meet Helen; but he staggered against a rock, and she saw that he
was completely exhausted—and no wonder!
Apart from the anxiety and remorse that he
had been enduring, he had not taken off his
clothes, had not slept, and had scarcely eaten,
for two nights and three days. He could

hardly speak, but clasped Helen's hand as though he found comfort in the pressure.

' How is she ?' he asked presently.

Helen knew whom he meant.

' She fainted, and seems only half conscious now. She walked and walked all day and night ; I thought she would go mad. Perhaps this breakdown is the best thing for her.'

' Yes, if only anyone could keep her unconscious. My God !' he groaned, ' it's too horrible !'

' The child ?' Helen asked. ' She will not go away from here till they have brought her.'

He gave a convulsive shudder.

' We had to bury her. It's too horrible—I can't tell her—she mustn't know. Can't you understand ? We couldn't bring it here. Death must have come the second day. We thought it might have been a snake-bite ; the body——' He broke off, shuddering again. ' I'm a strong man,' he said, ' and as a doctor I've seen bad sights ; but this one has utterly knocked me over, and you must forgive me.'

Helen was crying. The other men who had followed Geneste kept back. They had dismounted some little way off, and now quietly led their horses down the plateau to avoid startling the miserable mother by the sounds of their return. Helen looked for Tregaskiss: he was not amongst them. Geneste answered her unspoken question:

'The father? We left him—at the grave. He was stretched out upon it—he would not move—calling out for his Pickaninny. I' —he gave a sort of gulp—' I never in all my life felt so sorry for another man as I felt for Tregaskiss; and I never,' he added in a lower tone, turning away—' I never so hated myself.'

They walked down to the tent.

' I want to try and get a bit more like myself,' he said wearily. ' I—have something to give her—all that's left of the child. Helen, I think you must know what I feel— what she feels—the sting of it! It's best she should hear the worst from me. God help me to comfort her !'

A revulsion that was terrible in its intensity

45

came over Helen. Her heart had so gone
forth to him; she had so pitied him; she
had longed, like a sister, to console him. In
the tragedy of these last days she had almost
ceased to think of him as Mrs. Tregaskiss'
lover. And now—the thought of the father
stretched on his child's grave; the remem-
brance of what Gladys had told her of his
declaration that he was a changed man; and
then the picture of his wife, the bereaved
mother, consoled by—her lover! It was too
jarring—it was against Nature. Such things
had no right to be. And yet, through it all,
she loved him; and she had something of
the inconsistent mother-element mingling
with the love-element that there is in every
pure woman towards the man of her heart—
the mother-longing to snatch him from sin
and danger. At that moment she would
almost have laid down her life to save
Geneste from Clare Tregaskiss.

He felt the revulsion in her as she abruptly
moved from his side.

'Ah! you don't understand. You think it
abominable?'

She did not answer.

'It's all wrong,' he said ; 'yes, I know that. I've no right to expect that you would understand ; you are too good for that kind of thing.'

She left him without a word.

Clare Tregaskiss was sitting up in the cave when Geneste came to her. Gladys had met him at the entrance, and had left them to be alone together. She was sitting on a sort of couch they had made of piled-up blankets and leaves, in the recess where she and Ning were to have slept. The light, subdued by the half-drawn tarpaulin, and screened from her by a projecting piece of rock, was so dim, that at first he was hardly able to see the ravages which those awful days had made in her. Then, as he came closer and looked into her face, he was filled with a compunction so vast and overwhelming that for the moment it swallowed up the sense of their late relation to each other and all the more personal part of his love, so that there seemed no room for any emotion but that of immense pity. Her look terrified him. The lips were set in a travesty of her old still smile; her features were pinched and bloodless; her eyes started and burned out of red sockets. She was perfectly calm, but it was the calmness of frenzy.

'I am glad you have come,' she said as composedly as though she were receiving an ordinary visitor. 'It is quite fitting that you should be the one to tell me of my punishment, since it is through you that it has fallen upon me.'

Her manner frightened him. He made an inarticulate exclamation, and half stretched out his arms, but he dared not approach nearer.

'You see,' she went on, 'God has dealt me the full punishment. It is not only that He killed Ning, but He has given her to be devoured by the wild beasts, so that there is nothing of her I can keep even in memory. I can never think of her poor little face and her pretty soft limbs without seeing——'

Her voice hardly faltered, but a spasm of the muscles hindered her utterance. She closed her eyes, and for a moment he saw a wave of shuddering horror pass over her tense features. He groaned in anguish at her agony.

'Oh! how——' he began, and then could not put into words what she had divined.

'No one told me. I knew. That's what I was waiting for. I said to myself that if God gave me back the body of my child, it would be a sign to me that my sin would be forgiven. But, you see, there is greater retribution. I swore by my duty to my children. I have broken my oath, and I must pay the full penalty!'

'Clare—my poor darling! Your mind is unhinged with sorrow. You must not look upon this terrible thing which has befallen us in that light. Surely God is not less merciful than man. This is not retribution; it is not punishment for sin. There was no sin. The accident must have happened——'

'Do you know how it happened? There was no accident in it.' Her eyes through the dimness were like fires scorching him. 'I was sitting there waiting for you. I was thinking of you—only of you. I would not

listen to the child ; I would not look at her ;
she reminded me of her father. I told her
to go away. My last words to her were
angry words. Oh, dear Heaven ! did she
think of them when she called out to me in
her wanderings that night ? I put her out
of my mind all the time that you and I talked
of our love. Perhaps she was hesitating
then whether to go on further. Perhaps
while you held me in your arms and we
kissed each other she was saying to herself,
" Mummy doesn't want me." *I didn't want
her.* I was going to leave her altogether.
It was my thought that determined her to
wander on away from me. Our thoughts
are forces, moving people to do things.
Now it is all clear to me. When I gave you
that promise and threw away my cross, I
made it impossible for her to turn back.
She'd have come back if I hadn't thrown
away the cross. She'd have been saved if
only I had gone into the cave, for I should
have missed her—if I had only repented and
gone in. But I wouldn't go because I was
a guilty woman, and I didn't dare to look

into my child's innocent face. You know
I sat outside all the night. And I wouldn't
let myself think of her. I *wouldn't* listen
when she called to me—I could hear her
calling, and I told myself it was the curlews
—I hardened my heart. And I am a
wicked woman, and God has punished
me.'

She rose to her full height as she spoke,
and lifted her arms in a tragic gesture, which
told of the extremity of despair. Again he
was reminded of that gesture and wild cry
out into the lonely Bush night, 'How long,
O God! how long?' which had seemed to
him always somehow the very key-note of
Clare's inner life.

This gesture appeared to him one of dismissal—of repudiation; it awed him into
silence. He could not go close to her, or
even speak her name. He had a fancy just
then that she was not so much a woman to
be loved and comforted as a Fate announcing
her own doom. She went on, her voice like
molten metal dropping, never raised in tone,
but searing in its intensity.

'Now go! I don't want ever to see you again!'

'Clare!' he cried. 'Not like this! Oh, my darling, don't send me away like this!'

'Yes, go!' she repeated imperiously. 'What's the use of arguing and pleading? That will not change me. What's the use of piling on agony, either? How else do you want me to send you away? It won't make it easier to tell you that I love you. Do you need for me to tell you that? Haven't I done what proves it? Haven't I offered up my child and given myself to be accursed for love of you? That's enough. I've sworn before Heaven that never, as long as my husband lives, will I touch your hand again or willingly see your face. I shall not break *this* oath. So—good-bye.'

He stood silently imploring.

'Oh, go, go!' she cried again. 'Don't you hear me? You'll drive me mad standing there. Don't ever let me look at you again —that's all I ask. Put a barrier between us that neither can ever get over. Put the world between us—that would be best of all.'

'I will obey you,' he answered. 'Your will shall be my law, as I have always told you. You shall not be troubled by me. Good-bye—my dear—my dear, and may God help you in your misery! May He help us both!

He turned from her without another word, but paused and came back for a second, laying on a rock close by her something folded in a white handkerchief. The corners of the handkerchief fell apart and showed a child's little stained sock, a tiny discoloured boot, and a mass of dark brown curly hair.

CHAPTER XXXIII.

HUSBAND AND WIFE.

IT is the privilege of novelists and dramatists to loose the curtain-strings at the climax of a situation, and to let the drop-scene fall when emotions threaten to overpass the conventional limit. Real life, however, does not provide such convenient mechanism, and the human tragedy allows its performers no intervals of, so to speak, annihilation. Clare Tregaskiss had to live through days and weeks of dull hopeless pain; the climax passed, the tragedy played to the dying point, and then nothing left but the suspension of nerves and faculties in an aching blank of inaction. She was fortunate in this, that, though the suffering was acute all through the inaction, memory seemed, when it was over, to wipe a sponge over parts that had been most terrible. Looking back afterwards, she never knew how she had got through the journey from the Gorge to Darra-Darra, and thence, in Geneste's buggy, driven by Ambrose Blanchard, to her own home. She had refused to stay at Darra; and Geneste, in obedience to her command, had not accompanied her on that melancholy return ride from Lake Eungella. After that scene in the cave they had not met again. He had, indeed, put himself to a more refined martyrdom, by devoting himself to the service of Tregaskiss, who for days could not be induced to leave Ning's grave. It was the bereaved father who erected the sapling fence round the tiny mound, and with his own hands hewed the wooden cross that marked where the child's head lay.

Geneste knew that probably Clare would be very ill, now that the strain she had been undergoing was relaxed, and arranged with Mrs. Hilditch and with Blanchard, who had

learned something of doctoring in his ministra-
tions among the poor and his out-station and
diggings life, what to do in the event of the
crisis he dreaded, settling that they were to
send for him in case of serious emergency.
But Gladys Hilditch was aware of what had
passed in his last interview with Clare, and
determined within herself that, rather than
expose her friend to the danger of being
tended by Geneste, she would call up the
doctor from Port Victoria. For this, however, there was no need. Clare reached
Mount Wombo in a state of exhaustion,
which was, perhaps, a merciful palliative of
her mental pain. She lay for days as helpless
as a baby, the slightest exertion bringing on
a fainting fit and period of unconsciousness,
from which she emerged in a half-stupefied
condition, in which she noticed nothing, but
was apparently in no actual danger. Geneste
had warned Gladys against the probability of
these attacks, and had given her instructions
and provided her with restoratives, while a
black-boy in his employ kept up constant
communication between the two stations, so

that he was always informed of Mrs. Tregaskiss' condition.

They had been back a week before Tregaskiss returned. He did not say where
he had been or what he had been doing.
Certainly some great moral change had taken
place in him—a change which showed itself
also in his physical aspect. His face had
sharpened, and so looked more refined ; his
eyes were clearer, and his manner had lost
the boisterous brag which had made it so
objectionable. He was irritable, intensely
irritable, but this was a different sort of irrita-
bility from that with which his wife had been
familiar. Outside he found fault with the
men, swore at the black-boys even more than
of old, and denounced the drought and the
travelling mobs with all his former virulence;
but in the house he was curiously subdued,
would fall into long fits of moody silence even
at meals, when he would forget to eat, and
Gladys would sometimes see his eyes fixed
upon the chair that had been Ning's, and
which was now hidden away in an obscure
corner of the room ; or he would sit smoking

in the veranda for hours, never speaking,
with head bent and hands hanging listlessly,
his whole attitude expressive of such deep de-
jection that Gladys, much as she had disliked
her host, felt her heart go out to him in pity.
Sometimes the fits of silent smoking would
alternate with fierce trampings up and down,
the noise of which was the only thing that
roused Clare from her condition of semi-
stupor to some sign of sensibility. Indeed,
the fall of his footsteps got upon her nerves
so distressingly, that at last Gladys spoke to
Tregaskiss and begged him to desist.

He did not often go into his wife's room,
though he asked continually about her ; and
he sent a pack-horse to Ilganda for port wine
and other invalid delicacies, of which the
store was deficient. That penuriousness in
trifles, which had been an unpleasant trait in
his character, was not now so noticeable, and
the grudging of his wife's porter seemed
oddly coincident with over-indulgence on his
own part in 'nips.' Brandy is responsible
for many a squirk and extravagance, and
Philip drunk and Philip sober are always

different individuals. Tregaskiss appeared
to have manfully mastered his failing ; it was
evident that he had been thoroughly sincere
when he declared to Gladys that he was a
changed man. The sacrifice of Ning had
not been without its fruit on the outward
showing of things, which would seem to justify
the propitiatory theory and to prove that
martyrdom, even when it might be considered
useless, is the adjusting force in the great
universal scale, balancing good and evil.
From the time that he had dashed away the
pannikin of brandy and water, Tregaskiss
had never, to Gladys' knowledge, touched
spirits. She saw that he missed it horribly,
and was woman of the world enough to make
allowance on this score, as well as on that
of private grief, for his moody, ill-tempered
ways. She wondered within herself whether
he had made another kind of renunciation
likewise, and fancied that he must have done
so, for he never alluded to Miss Lawford as
he had before, in a sort of bravado, been in
the habit of doing, and never spoke of visiting Brinda Plains. She half suspected that

there had been a scene of final farewell and
of heroic resolve on his side in the interim
between Ning's death and his return to
Mount Wombo, and found something tragi-
cally comic in the notion of poor Tregaskiss
playing the chivalrous part.   Truly, the fact
was pathetic, if its workings were grotesque,
that Tregaskiss and his wife, at total variance
in nature and sympathies, should have been
acted upon by the same cause to arrive at
the same moral result.

After Gladys' remonstrance, Tregaskiss
tried to work off some of his misery on the
run.   He began the muster, which had been
delayed in the first instance because the
strike had called out the Bush workers,
drovers included, and it was not safe to start
fat cattle; and later in the hope of the
drought breaking up.   But day by day the
sun rose and set in pitiless glassy glare.   The
great plains grew browner and browner, and
the water-holes were patches of mud.   Even
the wiry gidia-trees seemed to droop and
shrink for want of moisture.   They were
cutting young trees to feed the cows, and

drawing water in buckets to give the beasts
drink.   More than one traveller was found in
the Bush dead of thirst; cattle and sheep
perished in hundreds and thousands, and ruin
was staring the poorer Leura squatters in the
face.

It was a bad time for Tregaskiss, hampered
as he was with debt.   The Bank had refused
to carry him on longer; he must make a large
sale or give up.   The Bank inspector had
come and gone while Clare was at her worst.
Moved to pity, perhaps by the desolation of
the house, he had made a hurried report and
had departed.   Now they were waiting to
know whether or not the station was to be
taken from them.

This was indeed a time of torture for a
sick woman.   The West in a rainy season
is bad enough; the West in a drought is
the Inferno.   It was terrible to lie there
under that heated zinc roof, the blinding
glare penetrating every crevice, and all the
contrivances for darkening the room only
excluding the gasped-for air.   Everything
the hand touched seemed to burn; metal

scorched ; the furniture, and even the buggy wheels, cracked and blistered ; the white ants swarmed ; mosquitoes and flies were in myriads ; and insects and reptiles came forth—the poisonous red spider, and centipedes and scorpions, a daily horror. Gladys sometimes marvelled that she herself lived through that time ; but love is an immense sustainer, and Blanchard was now continually at Mount Wombo. Over all hung the furnace-like heat and brooding stillness, only broken by dust-storms following a gathering of futile clouds—an irony in that parched land. Gladys prayed with the fervour of a devotee for rain. And at last a thunder-storm came. The running creeks put those at Mount Wombo in comparatively good spirits. The musterers started out, and at sundown the cracking of whips and bellowing of cattle announced their return. But the muster was a failure, the branding fell short of what had been expected, the cattle were too weak to travel ; and Tregaskiss sank again into irritable gloom. He had hardly been near his wife, and she had never asked for him. Both had the sense of an impending explanation, and both dreaded its happening.

It was brought about by the discovery which Tregaskiss made when turning over one day the documents in his safe, of that unfinished letter to Miss Lawford, directed to him in his wife's handwriting. He knew that Clare must have read the letter, and though it was not his way to take such incidents from the dramatic or emotional point of view, his slow imagination worked round the fact, and he felt that the letter might have largely influenced Clare's attitude towards him. He brooded aimlessly over the matter for several days during long lonely Bush rides, and then one afternoon, when he had got home earlier than usual from the run, without having any definite intention in his mind, he appeared on the upper veranda at the French window leading into her bedroom. She was sitting in a squatter's chair, between the draught of two windows, dressed in a white dressing-gown with deep black ribbons. The baby was playing on the floor at her feet, while Claribel waited outside in the veranda, crooning an aboriginal song. The sound exasperated Tregaskiss; it was the wild-duck ugal that Ning had been used to sing.

> 'Ya naia naringa,
>   Puanbu ni go
> Mingo ahikarai,
>   Whoogh !'

'Stop that infernal howling !' he cried out. 'How dare you sing that ? Be off, and take the child.' He picked up the baby and handed it to the half-caste. The little thing cried, and Clare moved uneasily. Tregaskiss turned to her with a sort of apology— his manner to his wife now was curious; it was sullen, but always deprecating and half ashamed. 'I'm sorry for the row,' he said. 'Those blacks' tunes drive me mad. Do you feel better, Clare ?'

'I'm going to get up and go downstairs to the dining-room to-morrow,' she answered. 'I am much better, thank you. I'm afraid you have been very uncomfortable, Keith !'

'Oh, I don't know. Gladys Hilditch looks after everything. She's a bit of a brick. By Jove! Blanchard's a lucky fellow. That engagement is a bad thing for us, though; she might have given us a helping hand.'

Clare winced.

'Oh, I don't think so,' she said vaguely.

'Where's old Cyrus Chance now?' asked Tregaskiss, with abruptness.

'I don't know if he has come back,' she answered. 'Jemmy Rodd told Gladys he was down South.'

'There's been a boom over one of his mines; and I see that shipment of meat has all gone off well. He must be coining money—adding millions to millions; and what good is it to himself or anybody? I've been thinking,' added Tregaskiss slowly, ' that if his liking for you is worth anything —and for——'

He paused, his face working.

Clare knew what was passing through his mind, and made a quick gesture of expostulation. Cyrus Chance had always been fond of Ning.   But to think of that fondness now as a marketable commodity choked her.

'You don't suppose I meant that?' Tregaskiss cried, interpreting the gesture with a quicker intuition than she had given him credit for.   He flung himself down upon a chair, and leant forward for a minute or two, his elbow on his knee, and his face buried in his hands.   Presently he looked up.   'It wouldn't go so much against the grain with me to ask the old miser anything now: that's all—because of—the Pickaninny.   I know he had an eye on this station when I first took it up, and that he has been watching the market; and Cusack told me he'd said he would buy it at his own price.   Well, I've been wondering if I could work a sale, and fix up the Bank.   The worst of it is that Chance is such an infernal screw, that he'd just wait till the Bank was down upon me, and then take it off their hands cheap.'

'I don't know,' said Clare dully.   'Do you want to sell the station, Keith?'

He gave a rough laugh.

'Wouldn't every man jack of us, on the

Leura, want to sell, if we could find a market? A drought isn't exactly selling time. But that's Cyrus's way of making money—buying in hard times, and selling in good ones. He can afford it. I'm in a tight place, as you know well enough, Clare, and if I can't do something, the place will be sold over our heads, and we shall walk out with nothing. I've had notice from the Bank. I didn't bother you, but I suppose you know that they sent an inspector up. Now, I thought you might help with old Cyrus— write a letter, ask him over here, or something that would give me a chance of breaking the ground. There's no use in my going over to him. He's such a queer fellow, he'd as likely as not, if he guessed my errand, send me to the huts.'

'I'll think about it, Keith. I couldn't ask him to lend money. But this isn't the same thing.'

'Very well. Jemmy Rodd will be passing by to-morrow.' Tregaskiss got up, as if he were going to leave her, but fidgeted about the room for a minute; then came back, and

again seated himself. 'Clare, I've got something to say to you. Do you think you are
strong enough to bear it ?'

'Yes,' she said faintly.

'Look here, we can't go on like this—
strangers in one house. We're husband and
wife still, when all is said and done, and
we've got to rough it along—the two of us—
somehow, even if you do hate me.'

'I don't hate you, Keith. I am very
sorry for having said those words ; they were
provoked.'

'Yes, I know they were,' he answered.
'And I've repented my part towards pro-
voking them, and humbly beg your pardon
for it. I had been taking more than was
good for me, Clare—that's the truth ; and I
was just mad that night, with one thing and
another. That's all past now. I didn't mean
what I said, and I'm glad you didn't mean
your words, either.'

'I had no right to say them, Keith. I
was sorry for you, even then. I am very
sorry for you now—sorry that you should be
tied to a woman like me, when you might be

so much happier with someone better suited to you. That's how I look at it.'

'Well, we've got to rough it along together somehow,' he repeated. 'And there's this to think of——' Tregaskiss' voice got husky again. 'The poor little Pickaninny belonged to both of us. And she was fond of her Daddy. You might forgive me, Clare, for her sake.'

'Oh, I forgive you—I forgive you utterly, if there's anything to forgive. But you don't know — it's I who ought to be forgiven——'

'Yes, I suppose I know—partly. Things seem to have got clearer in my mind ; they were all muddled before. I seem to see differently since the Pickaninny came to me that night—after—— I asked Mrs. Hilditch to tell you. Did she ?'

'Yes ; she told me.'

'I said I was a changed man, and it's true. You may have seen it—or perhaps Gladys Hilditch has told you that, too. I've not touched a drop of grog since that night, and I've made a solemn oath, by the child's grave,

that I'll never touch it again. That was the
root of it all. And it turned you against me,
and then I got mad, feeling I was a brute to
you, and that you despised me. It wasn't
that I didn't care for you, Clare. I've always
been fond of you, and I've always respected
you ; you've always kept your head above all
the Leura lot, and the fact is, you've been too
good for them—or me.'

Clare made an inarticulate murmur. The
great, blundering fellow went on :

'You are a different sort from women like
—like that poor little Hetty Lawford, for
instance. There was never anything really
wrong there—you must believe that, though
I was taken with her—and I'm fond of her
still—and I made a fool of myself. I know
you read that letter I began to her. I found
it the other day.'

'I would not have read it if I had known.
It was an accident, my coming across it. You
told me to go over the things in the safe. I
did not read it all—quite.'

'Well, that doesn't matter. You had a
right. I can understand that it made you

pretty sick over the whole business, and set you against me. I'm not defending myself. I was an ass, and my feelings carried me away. But I swear to you that there was nothing really wrong in it. You'll take my word of honour, won't you ?'

' Yes, Keith, I believe you.'

' It's all done with. I don't want ever to see her again. She cared for me a bit, poor little thing! I don't want to say a word of her that isn't good ; she doesn't deserve it. I've seen her, and told her that it's all over and done with, and I expect she'll end by marrying that old Land Commissioner. I've advised her to, and to get away from the Cusacks. We've all been on the wrong track, and it's time we took new bearings.'

' Will you take me away ?' she asked wildly. ' If you can only sell the station, will you take me right away ?'

' That's what I want. I'll take you to a cooler climate, and where you won't have such a rough life, even if we can but just scrape enough out of Mount Wombo to hire a cottage South—on the Ubi, perhaps ; you'd

like that ? And we'll begin afresh. Will
you agree to that, Clare, for the sake of the
poor little dead Pickaninny ?'

Then, almost for the first time since Ning
died, the woman's stony reserve gave way.
She cried as if her heart were breaking, trying to get out words of self-reproach and of
entreaty for forgiveness—trying to make him
understand the agony of humiliation his
trust in her created, half repulsing his efforts
to soothe her, yet humbly grateful for the
dog-like, tentative caresses which were all he
dared offer. By-and-by she sobbed out :

'Oh, Keith ! if you knew, you wouldn't
be like that. If you knew how bad I have
been !'

'I don't want to know,' he answered
stolidly. 'I dare say you were led away,
as I was myself. Of course I knew Geneste
was in love with you. But I know that
nothing would have ever made you forget
your dignity, Clare, and your duty as a wife
and a mother.'

'No !' she cried, pierced to the soul. 'I
can't let you think that of me, when it isn't

true—when I am a wicked woman, whom God has punished for her sin! I had promised to go away,' she said in a very low voice. ' I was determined to throw up everything. I meant to leave you for ever —you and the children !'

She sat like a criminal, with her head bent. She could not meet her husband's eyes, which she felt were fixed upon her. Yet there was a sense as of a load lifted when she had made her confession. She heard him utter a choking sound, as though he were trying to speak, but could not get out the words. There was a long silence. At last he said hoarsely :

' You can go if you like, Clare. I have no right to keep you, or expect you to live with me. I've cared for you tremendously, and I do care for you still, though you may not believe it. I came here honestly meaning to beg your forgiveness, and to ask you to let us begin a new life. But, if it's like that, and you'd rather go, I'll not say anything, and I'll get a divorce, and you can marry him. You can take the baby if you like. I don't

care for her.   I don't care for anything now
that Ning's gone.   I don't care what becomes
of me.   I'd as soon as not go and cut my
throat and be done with it.'

She looked up at him in wonder and a
kind of awe.   He was gazing straight out
of the window with an expression upon his
face she had not believed it possible he could
wear.   She saw that he had not spoken
in anger or resentment — that he meant
what he said—and she began to wonder
dimly whether, in truth, there were depths in
poor Tregaskiss' nature which she had never
sounded.

'Well ?' he said at length, still not looking
at her.   'Do you want to go ?'

'No, Keith,' she answered, in a clear,
decided voice.   'I am going to stay with you,
and do my best to make up for what's gone
by, if you will let me.'

After that conversation with Tregaskiss,
Clare began to get better, and asked to get
up.   Presently she took up again the ordinary
duties of her life in a strange, silent way,

never alluding to her loss, and avoiding mention of Geneste. It made Gladys' heart ache to see how watchful she was of her baby, hardly allowing it, with Claribel, out of her sight, and how she attended to every little detail of housekeeping, getting up early to do her dairy work, making and mending, and giving out rations, as she had been used to do. Except that she never laughed, and that the smiling curve of her lips was set into an expression of exquisite apathy, she did not seem very different from the still, reserved, sweet woman of a few months before.

'There's just this difference,' said—in answer to a remark by Gladys—Helen Cusack, who had ridden over one day with Ambrose Blanchard. 'She was alive before, and now the best part of her is dead.'

Helen's eyes followed Mrs. Tregaskiss in wistful questioning, and with a certain awed wonder. Had the strongest thing in her really died with Ning? Did she still love Geneste?

They were sitting in the upper veranda
the evening before Helen went home again,
when Clare, turning to her suddenly, said,
for the first time mentioning Geneste's
name :

' Do you ever see Dr. Geneste ?'

Helen went red, though in the dimness of
the veranda it was not noticeable, and hesitated as she answered :

' Yes ; he comes over sometimes.'

' Why has he not gone to England ?'

Helen faltered more.

' I—don't know.'

' Will you tell him,' continued Clare quite
calmly, ' that I think he ought to go soon,
unless he has made up his mind to marry and
settle down on the Leura.   He ought to
marry, tell him, and have children and a real
home.   It is a great pity that he should
waste his life as a bachelor, when he might
make some good, sweet girl very happy,
and be very happy himself.   He ought to
go to England and take up his profession
again.   Please give him that message from
me.'

'Mrs. Tregaskiss,' said Helen, 'will you not see him and tell him that yourself?'

'No, my dear,' she answered quietly; 'I do not wish ever to see Dr. Geneste again— at any rate, not for a great many years. He reminds me of what made the keenest agony in my great sorrow, what has changed me into another woman from the Clare Tregaskiss he used to know. That Clare he will never know again. Tell him that, too, please; he will understand.'

It was not very long after this that Jemmy Rodd brought Mrs. Tregaskiss two letters. The first she opened was from Geneste. It had no formal beginning or ending, and this was what he said:

'I am obeying you. You told me that you never wished to see my face again; you bade me place a barrier between us which neither could ever pass over. I have done so. I am going to marry Helen Cusack, and we shall shortly leave for England together. I am not worthy of her, but she knows all that I could honourably disclose, and accepts me as I am—a man, no nobler, no truer than many another man. She loves me far more than I deserve, and to me she is so dear that it will be my best happiness to try and make her happy. Good-bye. I understand you, and I pray God to bless you.'

The second letter was from Cyrus Chance, and ran thus :

'MY DEAR MISTRESS TREGASKISS,

'I have but just come from one of my sugar plantations, after being down on the Ubi, to learn, to my great astonishment and grief, of the sad misfortune that has befallen you. I will say no words, for I was fond of the wee thing ; and deeds will speak plainer, as you will learn. I got your letter about the station ; and on that matter I will treat with your husband, for ladies are best left out of business. I like the place, and I'm disposed to go a small bit above the market value, which is next to nothing just now. But only a small bit, mind you, so don't let him think he can pile it on. A gift's a gift, and a deal's

a deal. I have no opinion of him as a
manager, or I would offer him the billet. If
he'll take advice from me, he'll go South, and
start as a stock and station agent, where his
habit of blowing will come in useful. I hear
he has given up nipping, and I'm glad of it,
and hope he'll continue temperate. I have
seen young Blanchard, and have heard a
great deal from him about his own and othei
people's matters. The man is straight ; and
since " Fair Ines " had to make a fool of herself and come down to be just like the rest of
you, she might have done it worse ; but she
had better have stopped in Dreamland, which
is where I shall always think of her.

'About yourself. I have watched you for
a long time, and old man Chance saw deeper
down below things than you have any idea.
He saw into your heart, for all that he is a
woman-hater, and never had a woman in the
world that loved him, nor loved one himself,
unless it's you, dear Mistress, and my dream-
woman, "Fair Ines." So I know that you have
had a trouble eating your heart all the while ;
and I am sorry for you, and glad to know now

that it has ended in the only right way it could end. You remember what I said to you a while ago: "Nurse your babies, and turn them into blessings." You've got your little one left, and though it will never be like the one God has taken—for she was a rare and gracious creature—it will be something for you to love and cherish when all else has failed.

'And now I come to the deed I spoke of, which is just this : When I went home after that day that I saw you in your pretty drawing-room, furnished so cheaply and so comfortable, with the two babies by you, and Ning so sweet and pretty, I made a codicil to my will, by which I left your Ning that's gone £20,000, to be held by you in trust for her if I died before she was of age, and to come to you afterwards if the baby died first. This day I have put that amount in the hands of trustees, as a settlement upon yourself ; the lawyers will put it all into proper words and do the rest ; and I wish you to consider it, not as a gift from me, but as your rightful inheritance from your

dead child.   You will find, placed quarterly
to your credit at the Bank of Leichardt's
Land, due interest for the same.

'God bless you, Mistress Tregaskiss, is
the prayer of your friend and well-wisher,

'CYRUS CHANCE.

'P.S.—I suppose you know that Geneste
is going to marry Helen Cusack, and young
Gillespie has gone South, looking awful
down-in-the-mouth.'

THE END.

BILLING AND SONS, PRINTERS, GUILDFORD.

www.ingramcontent.com/pod-product-compliance
Lightning Source LLC
Chambersburg PA
CBHW030808020726
47499CB00006B/1819